ELPHANY

Cathy A. Walters

authorHOUSE®

AuthorHouse™
1663 Liberty Drive
Bloomington, IN 47403
www.authorhouse.com
Phone: 1-800-839-8640

First published by AuthorHouse   11/14/2011

ISBN: 978-1-4670-3497-5 (sc)
ISBN: 978-1-4670-3498-2 (ebk)

Library of Congress Control Number: 2011916461

Printed in the United States of America

Tarah

Tarah sat there starring into the pond at herself. She couldn't believe that her uncle kept saying she was so beautiful.

Her eyes were blue like the sky and sparkled like the stars. Her hair was golden blonde like the sun. And it flowed past her ankles. She had to put it in a bun so it wouldn't drag on the ground and get dirty.

Her uncle Remus made her promise to never cut her hair. From time to time he would remind her of her promise.

She would always ask him why and all he would say was, when you are old enough I will tell you everything you need to know.

She was sitting there crying she knew her uncle couldn't take anymore of those beatings and she knew he was going to die, and there was nothing she could do about it.

He was the only person in her life since the age of five. When she was separated from her parents.

She felt helpless and devastated. Knowing her uncle couldn't take much more of the beatings from the hunters. They had been sent by the wizard Nevis to take her back to him and her uncle would make her hide every time until they left. What she didn't know is why they wanted her.

She wanted to kill them for what they were doing to her uncle.

She stood up and started looking for her best friend Succoth. He was a red and blue striped tiger. Which was very common on the planet Pholigue. There were three suns and five moons. The planet was so beautiful the woods had trees that had decorations of different colored leaves which were blue, green, turquoise, orange pink and red. The trunks of the trees grew out of the ground and they were rainbow colored.

The stream was blue like the sky and so clear you could see all the way to the bottom.

There was a waterfall across the stream that had a cave behind it. Where all the animals would go when there was bad weather.

The grass was multicolored with a brilliance of flowers and plant life all around it. It was like the woods was keeping watch over her.

Tarah had different whistles for all the animals in the woods.

She looked around and seen all her animal friends gathering around her in a circle. There was a pink deer, a bear that was blue and white, rabbits who were multicolored., birds of many colors foxes that were blue and gray, and horsed of multicolor.

Tarah looked at all them and started crying again. It saddened her to have to tell them she was going to leave them. She didn't want to leave this was the only home she'd ever known.

This was the only home she had ever known. I don't want to have to leave any of you. But I know and all of you know I must leave soon. However she made a promise that she would try to come back for them.

There is so much I need to do before those hunters come back. This time and they are going to pay for what they are doing to me and my uncle.

If only I would have let them take me she thought, then her uncle would not be in this trouble. What did they want with me? She asked.

Then her fear would take over she needed someone to hold her and tell her everything was going to be alright.

Her uncle forbid her from having any contact with another person, he didn't trust anyone around either of them.

Now what was she going to do if he died. Now he is going to have to tell me everything or take it to his grave.

She was not sure if she was ready to know the truth. So many things were going through her head.

She knew that she was going to have to be brave for she had a very dangerous and exciting path ahead of her.

If she ever going to get to the bottom of this secret.

She whistled again. Her uncle kept telling her she had a very special talent and she was just like her mother.

He loved her so much. He told her all the time she was so pure and innocent and wished she could stay that way for the rest of her life.

After awhile Tarah was ready to whistle again wondering why Succoth was taking so long to come back.

Where those hunters at the cabin still? She asked herself.

Succoth came up from behind her. He was such a beautiful animal and very protective of her.

He was playfully trying to sneak up on her, when she sensed his presence as he was ready to pounce on her she moved turned around and looked at Succoth and knew the hunters were gone. I am sorry my friend just cannot play right now. There is so much I need to do before those hunters come back. In addition I want to be ready for them this time they will pay for what they had done to her uncle.

She started walking then took off running with Succoth right beside her all the way.

She really needed to talk to her uncle before it was to late.

She looked at Succoth and said. If I have to go away you are going with me I will never leave you behind. I love you to much and you are the closest friend I have. I couldn't imagine my life without you and my uncle in it.

Succoth knew from the very start that he was going with her even if she told him he could not. H e had made a vow to himself that he would protect her till the day he died.

When they reached the cabin Succoth took off ahead to stand guard in the shadows. Just in case the hunters cane back so he could warn her ahead of time.

Tarah walked into the cabin and looked around for her uncle, she saw that he was sleeping in his bed, so she went into the kitchen. He needed to rest. She decided that she would cook dinner. She knew they both were going to need all the strength they could to battle with those hunters the next time they came back. And she wasn't going to hide next time they come back.

Just as she was about to start dinner Tarah heard a frail voice that came from her uncle.

Asking is that you Tarah? We need to talk while I still have a breath left in me. She turned around and walked towards him, surprised that he was awake.

Yes uncle Remus it is I Tarah. Will you bring me a glass of water? He asked. Tarah went to the sink and got the water, went back held his head up to help him drink. When he was done she put the glass on the nightstand, got down on her knees and took his hands in hers. Anxiously waiting for him to tell her the secret that plagued her all her life.

Uncle Remus looked at her with the most loving eyes and said, You are a woman now Tarah and you innocent beauty and pure heart will change the whole universe.

There will be many men who will ask for your hand in marriage. However there is only one special man out there that your will give your whole heart and soul to. And when you make love your souls will entwine into one.

Now I need to tell you what has happened to your parents and when it all began.

Although Tarah wanted to know about what he was saying about the man she would fall in love with and she was a little stunned cause he forbid he to have any human contact whatsoever. But she was anxious to hear what he had to say.

Finally, he said do you remember when you first came here? I was to protect you; You were just five years old at the time. Now you are eighteen and enough to go out in the world and its not going to be easy at first. However you are strong willed in everyway. And the love that you have inside of you will be shown to others by just your touch. When you gently move your hand on my face I can feel the love pour out from you. Remus said. You are one of the chosen ones that will live longer then anther being on this planet or any other planet you go to. People will treat you as if you are a goddess.

Tarah just sat there stunned, Now she really had questions to ask. She started to say something but he didn't stop talking, I have to tell you this now then I will answer all your questions. He went on, you will never look any older then you are now you are a very beautiful woman.

You see those hunters that were here looking for you and have been coming twice a year over the years.

But now that you have turned into a very beautiful woman. They are more determined then ever to find you.

You must never let them catch you. You have to be alert at all times.

And you have the ability to sense if a stranger comes up to you that you can trust.

If they do catch you they will take you to the wizard Nevis; do not ever look into his eyes for if you do he will suck all the life out of you as you know now.

Tarah just sat there starring at him in disbelief. She didn't know what to say or do.

Go to the fireplace third one down on the right side tap on the brick twice. Remus told her.

When Tarah did a brick slid open revealing a secret compartment. When she looked inside there was a small jewelry box in there and a black velour bag with a gold cord on it. Remus told her to remove them from their hiding place. Then he told her to tap once on the brick and it slid back into place. She took the box and the back over to her uncle. Open the jewelry box. Remus said. When she opened it, Tarah found a thick gold chain with a big round deep red garnet pendant hanging from the chain, she picked it up to admire it more closely.

To her surprise it was a locket. Remus told her to open it. When she did the memories starting flooding

Back her heart started aching and tear welled up in her eyes. Her father was a ruggedly handsome man with brown eyes and long black wavy hair that was tied back with a bow.

And dressed in handsome attire. And her mother was dressed in a white flowing gown with flowers sewn on it she had long golden blonde hair. Blue eyes and a smile that could warm your heart As she looked at her mother it was as if she was looking into a mirror at herself. These are my parents aren't they? She asked Remus.

Yes he said they were very much in love and they still are as far as I know and wonderful parents which they loved you very dearly. Now they need your help.

Tarah took a deep breath and wondered why they left her behind in addition where are they now?

Why hadn't they contacted her all these years? Her uncle kept talking it was as though he couldn't get the words out fast enough. I know you have a lot of questions but first I need to finish telling you what you need to know and as I talk you will have all the answers.

Remus told her to put the chain on and never take it off ever. This will help you when danger comes along. As she put the locket on he went on saying this is no ordinary locket then instructed her to push on the back of the locket with her thumb while holding and pointing the jewel. When she did a bolt of lightening shot from the jewel.

It hit the dresser and put a hole in it. Tarah starred in amazement. She could not believe what had just happened. Then Remus told her to tug on the chain, when she did she felt a little tingle go through he body.

He said if anyone touches the chain they will get a full jolt and knock on the ground.

Look into the jewelry box again and you will find two more chains. One goes on your wrist and the other goes around your ankle. Tarah put them on.

He went on to tell her when your parents brought you to me, they said that you have your mothers powers and you would learn how to use them from your animal friends.

Tarah seemed to be able to hear their thoughts and Succoth taught her how to fight. She had a sense all of her life that she was on a special mission. Only she had no idea what it was going to be. Her uncle had been preparing her for this for all these years for something she was going to have to do, now she was finally going to find out what it was.

Tarah, Tarah, Tarah her uncle kept calling her name. it was as if she was someplace else. After about the fourth time Tarah finally looked up form the bracelet she was rolling around her wrist. And asked why haven't you mentioned any of this to me before?

Because I have been preparing you for this moment and you needed to be old enough to handle the responsibility of what I am going to tell you. Then he went on to tell her that the bracelet will turn you invisible and will send you anywhere you want to go. However you must not tell anyone about this unless you are sure you can trust that person.

In addition my dear you will know when you can trust them. You have a natural ability to know who to trust. Then he said take the and bracelet off and stretch it out. When she did the chain turned into a staff. It was as long as her arm. Remus reached his arm out touched it and said this is what you will be using for self defense.

Succoth will help you learn how to use it. However I have a feeling you will not need it. Then he told her to push both ends of the staff at the same time. When she did it turned back into a bracelet she then put it back on her ankle.

Tarah looked at her uncle he looked so pale and old. She asked him if he wanted to rest. He shook his head no, I will rest after I tell you everything.

Tarah stood up and started pacing the floor. Please sit down Tarah there isn't much time left. Tarah started crying. Oh uncle Remus why does it have to happen to you. She went over and gave her uncle a hug. Uncle Remus put his arm around her now, now Tarah everything will be alright.

Please sit down he asked her so I can tell you more. Tarah let go of her uncle, tears falling from her eyes. How long have I had these powers? She asked wiping her tears away.

Some of the powers you have had all your life. The others you didn't have till you put the jewelry on.

Then uncle Remus said never cut your hair for if you do you will grow old and die like everyone else. that's what keeps you and your mother alive and looking young.

Tarah looked at her uncle, what about my father, is he going to live forever? If he never stray's from your mother he will live forever too. However if they are away from each other for a long period of time he will grow old and die. He answered. Tarah put her hands on her face and started crying again. I must help them get back home. she said.

Now my dear child you must not cry. As he patted her arm. I know you wondered why you parents have left you here as they did when you were very young. Its hurts me so not to tell you all these years. But I was sworn to secrecy and your parents lives depended on it. They have been gone for thirteen years now. I hope and pray you will understand my keeping this from you for so long. I just could not tell you any of this until now.

There is a man out there and his name is Nevis and he sent your parents to another planet far, far away from here until he has your hand in marriage. Tarah started to get up until her uncle grabbed her arm and yelled in a deep voice. No! Tarah I forbid you to marry him. Tarah looked at him in amazement. He had never ever talked to her like that before. His eyes were filled with fear and pain.

But uncle Remus if I can get my parents back home why cant I marry him?

Because if you do that there is no stopping him from getting what he wants from the whole universe and that isn't what you want. You are so full of love and happiness. That is how I raised you. So please do not ever think of marrying Nevis. He will destroy everything and everyone that gets in his way. Remus told Tarah.

I do not understand why is he so cold, has he ever known what love is? Tarah asked.

He was not that way when he was younger. Remus said. Once when he was seventeen he very much in love and he was ready to marry a woman that he loved more then life himself. However he was called off to fight a battle to save his kingdom. When he came back he found that his soon to be bride was already married to another man. She was very hurt for she thought that Nevis was dead when he was gone for so long. Nevis was so angry he would not let her explain anything to him. He just stormed off yelling back saying they were going to pay for all the heartache that they had caused.

You see Tarah that woman was your mother. When your father came along it took him almost a year to get your mother to go out with him. She was very much in love with Nevis and couldn't see herself with anyone else.

When your father finally won her heart they were inseparable not long after that you were born.

Nevis studied all kinds of magic and when he was good at it. He figured out how to ban your parents to another world. When your mother found out what he was going to, she feared for your life and brought you to me.

If Nevis would have gotten to you first he would have locked you up until you were old enough to marry him. Then work his evil on the universe. You were so young at the time and the spitting image of your mom.

I promised your parents I would take care of you and teach you how to use your powers. This is why those hunters keep coming back. However, they could never find you thanks to the watchful eyes of the animals.

That is why I had to keep you hidden from Nevis. Remus said.

I am so lucky to have you and all these animals around me. Am I the only one that can stop him? Tarah asked. I cant answer that for you, you are the only one that can. Remus said.

Then that is what I must do, Tarah said.

Remus to the bag from Tarah and opened it, pulled out a piece of paper and unfolded it. This is a map to the wizards palace. It is a long and dangerous journey, you must watch every step you take. If you should be approached by the wizard or the hunters make yourself invisible fast. And wish yourself to be someplace else. Remus said.

I will I promise uncle Remus. I am doing this all for you and my parents. Tarah said.

Remus pulled out another piece of paper. This is the deed to your parents palace, they gave it to me to hold for you. He handed it to her with another paper that was a map attached to it. It was tattered and yellowed from age. When you arrive there you will find a man named Joshua, the butler. He will assist you on anything you need. He was a very loyal to your parents and he still is. Your parents treated him like he was part of the family. Just like everyone else that came into their life. He will never do anything to betray you and your family. And he knows the palace inside and out. Remus said.

This will come in handy, it was another map that was yellowed and tattered. This will show you where your worldly possessions are. You are the richest person in the universe. You will never have to want or go without ever again. You will have cuts and bruises along the way and much heartache, but in the end when this is all over then hopefully the evil in Nevis will be defeated. It will be better for all the people in the universe. And you will be stronger for this. Remus said.

Remus reached in the bag and pulled out another small light blue bag, this is sleeping powder, use it sparingly until you get to your palace. Then Joshua will give you all you need. He said.

Be very careful when you get to your palace for Nevis has the hunters staked out all over the place. Then he reached in the black bag again and pulled out a red bag, this powder you will use on the hunters. The wizard put a spell on them, and this will take away the spell. Therefore you will have to get to them first by blowing the powder in their face one by one. In addition you will have to get all of the hunters before you can get to the wizard.

The wizard is a very cruel and devious man and will stop at nothing to get what he wants. Remus told Tarah.

Tarah just sat there starring at her uncle, wondering how she was ever going to stop the wizard. In a way she didn't like the wizard for what he had done to her parents, but in another she felt compassion. For him love had turned into hate and a broken heart can make you numb inside and turned your heart into stone. She decided first to try and change that and if that didn't work the she would have to defeat him.

Remus went on to say, on the way to your palace you will meet people along the way, ask them their name. if their name is not Shavouth then blow the powder in their face and run off. Shavouth will help you find the way to the wizards palace. He will be your knight in shining armor. When her uncle emptied the bag and finished explaining the contents. He put them all back in the same way he had taken them out, and handed it back to her.

Then he went on saying that you have more powers inside of you but only you will know what they are.

Remus asked her to go to the closet on the right side of the fireplace, remove the strange looking garment with a cap pinned on it. There is a cape hanging next to it. When she did he told her to go to her room and put it on.

As she went to her room to change, she wondered what she would look like in the suit. All she had ever worn was dresses. And it looked so different. She started to protest about the outfit. But Remus insisted and she gave up after a little persuasion. To her surprise Tarah looked really good in the outfit. She went downstairs and told her uncle she looked more like a boy then a girl.

Yes I know that is why I made the suit. If you were to go out without the suit on you would surely be caught before you get to the wizards palace. So wear that suit at all times. Remus said.

Tarah looked at her uncle. He looked very pale and tired. We have been talking for most of the day and it's starting to get dark out. Don't you think you should rest to get your strength back? She asked.

There are a few more things I need to tell you, then I will rest. He answered.

Tarah sat down and grabbed his right hand. Your hand is very cold do you need a blanket? She asked.

Remus shook his head no so Tarah sat there to listen.

Remus went on you are the only person that has kept me going all these years, now that its almost time for me to go, God is waiting for me to go with. I have done all I can for you now its up to you now.

Please do not make a wish to keep me alive forever. God is the one that gave you this gift and if and he can take it away. If he does you will die and all hope is lost.

Tarah promised her uncle she wouldn't go against god's wishes with tears in her eyes.

I do not know where Nevis has banned your parents to, all I know is that it is a planet far away behind the stars. The only way to find them is through the wizard or to find out where he does his magic, which will be in or around his palace. Or destroy the evil inside him.

If it ever comes down to where you have to destroy the planet there is a spaceship hidden on the grounds of your palace. Take as much of your fortune as will fit in the spaceship as you can. You will be able to use them wherever you go. Tarah got up to make some supper and hot tea for the both of them. She could have wished for it but she needed to get up and move around. Remus looked up at her and said why don't you go lay down for awhile after we eat.

She shook her head yes and started yawning. After fixing dinner, helping her uncle eat while she ate at the same time she sat there thinking about what laid ahead of her.

Remus put his tea on the night stand and tried to get up, Tarah helped and grabbed his cane that was hanging on the bedpost and handed it to him. After he walked into the bathroom and closed the door.

Tarah got down on her knees and started praying. Please god let uncle Remus die in peace with no pain he has suffered enough. And please help me stop that evil man.

And give him a good place there with you he his a great man. And please help me stop that evil man and all the evil that's out there. Amen.

Tarah sat back down in the rocker grabbed her tea and started sipping on it, she felt drained this is a lot for a young woman to take in when she was raised not knowing about her parents and not knowing what lay ahead of her.

Uncle Remus walked out of the bathroom slowly, he was white as a ghost, looked at Tarah and said I don't think I can make it to the bed. Can you help me? He asked.

Tarah sat her tea down and went and helped Remus into bed. Handed him his tea. He drank a little more of it put it on the nightstand, then laid back down. He looked up at Tarah, please do not be sad my dear child, I will always be there to guide you when you need me the most. Remus told Tarah. Now please go to bed and get some sleep Succoth will let us know if those hunters come back.

Tarah stood up, gave her uncle a kiss on the cheek. I will never forget you uncle you are the only father I have ever known I love you dearly.

Tarah went upstairs. To get some sleep. Thinking of what her uncle had told her. Asking herself why am I the one that is chosen to do this? What if I can't stop the wizard. However for the love of my family I will do what needs to be done. I will take this journey wherever it may take me. I promise you uncle Remus I will capture the wizard and I will break that cold heart of his. Tarah fell asleep after an hour of tossing and turning.

Meanwhile Remus was laying there. Please god help my Tarah get through this follow her and protect her.

At that time a hand reached down and gently grabbed Remus by the hand. When Remus looked up it was the hand of god and in a soft voice god told Remus it is time to come be with me you have done good in this life come be with me now and you shall never feel pain anymore. Remus closed his eyes and walked with god.

About two hundred miles away the wizard sat by himself at the big dining table eating his dinner, when the hunters walked in.

The wizard looked up at them and asked have you found her yet?

No but we know she is there. We saw the table set for two people. Therefore she was not far. One of the hunters answered.

How does she know when you are coming? The wizard asked.

Both hunters shrugged at the same time. We do not know. The wizard looked at and said you two go after her, I want her back within two weeks. If you come back alone I will destroy the both of you and your family. Do you understand. The wizard looked up at them.

I will have you as my bride Tarah, one way or another you will be mine. Shaking his fists in the air. The wizard said.

There is on more thing master. One of the hunters said.

The wizard looked at him anger started pouring out of him. What is it now? My dinner is getting cold.

Its about Remus. This last beating we gave him. I think he is dying from it. We were really rough on him this time. They said.

11

Good The wizard said. Now Tarah is going to be more vulnerable then ever with her uncle out of the way. Started laughing it sounded so evil. I will finally have what is rightfully mine. He smiled a wicked smile that made the hunters cringe in fear. Stood up from the table looked at both the hunters now go get her and don't come back alone.

The hunters bowed to the wizard when he stood up. They wondered why he had so must hate built up inside of him. They could not understand. All they knew was to bring the girl back. Or they would die.

As they walked out the door they heard him laugh and it brought shivers down their spine.

After they left the wizard started pacing the floor saying to himself why did you betray me Elphany? I loved you so much and you betrayed me. He raised his fists in the air I shall ruin everything and everyone she has ever loved starting with your daughter Tarah.

The wizard left the dining room, went upstairs to his bedroom, walked over to the mirror across from the bed pushed on a panel right above the frame of the mirror. The wall moved inward and he went inside. With the wall closing behind him.

The wizard walked about twenty feet to a rocky staircase went up them. Pulled a skeleton key out of his pocket and unlocked the door. The door creaked when he opened and shut it.

Then walked over to the table in the middle of the room that had vials, goblets, different colored stones, jars full of weird looking thins in them and books of magic spells. Then went over to the right side of the table on the wall he grabbed the cape and cap and put them on.

The wizard left the room locking the door behind him, went down the stairs through his bedroom.

Then he went out side to the back where the garden was. Walked down a path to where his spaceship was. Opened up a panel on the right side of the spaceship, pushed in order, red, blue, yellow and green. A door slid into the wall as it did the wizard stepped back and waited for the must smell to leave. As soon as it was gone he went inside turned around and opened anther panel pushed the same buttons but in a different order.

He looked around and seen that everything was the same as he left it. He then walked over and sat down in a chair. Turning the chair around he could see another door that led to a corridor which led to other rooms on the spaceship.

When he had the chair positioned. He started pressing about ten different buttons. The spaceship started making noises and then the engines kicked on. Buckled himself in the chair and pushed about four more buttons. The spaceship lifted up off the ground and took off into space. Set the quarter nets of where he wanted to go. Unbuckled his seatbelt sat back in his seat and relaxed. Then said aloud. I shall go to Elphany and that darling husband of hers and let them know of the good news. Then I shall return for my special occasion. He laughed an evil laugh that echoed throughout the spaceship. Then closed his eyes and went to sleep. After the wizard slept for a few hours he woke up hungry got up went to the kitchen to see if there was anything to eat. Found some jars of food opened them and ate out of the can he didn't know how to cook so he ate his food cold.

After a week went by he finally made it to his destination. He went back and sat in his chair buckled up and pushed more buttons to land the ship he found a nice little spot by some woods. To land it. Shut it down, unbuckled himself, got up and stretched his arms and legs. Walked towards the hatch opened it and slowly stepped outside looking around to see if anyone was there. Then he started circling the ship sprinkling dust around at the same time. Except for a little area so he could find the spaceship.

He looked around and said so this is what you call earth. It is much different then Pholigue.

There was trash blowing in the wind. And there was and an unusual odor to it to. The wizard frowned if only Elphany wouldn't have done me wrong, she would still be by my side, then the anger flared up in him again.

He looked down at his wrist band, pushed some buttons and located where Elphany would be at when his wrist band started beeping it showed a map and the name of a town called timber creek.

He took his compass out and it pointed in the direction he needed to go.

As he was walking he was searching for the right words to say. Hoping he would not say the wrong thing when he seen Elphany. He watched cautiously to see if anyone was watching him.

After the wizard walked a good ten miles, he finally came to a town. He looked behind him a few blocks and seen someone walking. He ducked behind a bush till the person went by. As he was watching the person pass by he seen the clothes the person was wearing and looked down at his. Well this wont do I will surely be spotted now. So he looked behind him and saw a clothesline went to it and grabbed some clothes that looked like they would fit him. Put them on. Wrapped the cape and others together and tucked them under his arm.

Then took off towards the town called Timber Creek. He was walking down the road when he heard a strange noise come up behind him and stopped. The wizard was getting angry he didn't know what to do.

He seen the car door open and a tall stocky man climbed out of the vehicle and started walking toward him.

The man yelled stop police. The wizard stopped.

The police officer walked up to him and asked him why he was walking down the middle of the road so late in the night.

Can I see some identification the policeman asked. Looking at him suspiciously.

The wizard looked at him funny sorry sir I lost it. Then what is your name the policeman asked.

Nevis the wizard answered.

Why are you doing out here this late. The wizard looked at the policeman and looked at the vehicle and said. I broke down so I started walking so I could get to my relatives house. That lives in Timber Creek.

Well I am going that way can I give you a ride. The police officer said. The he asked what their names were.

Then the wizard had to think what the name was that Elphany was going by.

Then it clicked and he said Mr. and Mrs. Joe Sherman. They live somewhere in the country.

The policeman was getting more suspicious on what the wizard was doing there and he could sense it.

Then they came to the edge of town and the wizard said here is the place pointing to the left side of the road it was a small white house with brown shutters on it.

He had to get out of the car before the policeman found out why he was there.

As the policeman pulled off to the side of the road he knew the people that lived in the house. Put the car in park and said are you sure you don't have any kind of identification on you.

The wizard said let me look I may have something here. He reached in his cape and grabbed a handful of dust out of a bag. And blew it at the policeman.

Before the policeman realized what he was doing and started to grab for his pistol, it was to late he was fast asleep.

The wizard checked and the policeman was fast asleep. Good he will sleep for a few hours now. He pulled the policeman out of the vehicle and laid him on the road, looked around and no one was around. Then quickly changed outfits with him.

The uniform and shoes wear a little big but he had to make the most of what he had for the time being.

The put the police officer in the back seat then climbed in the drivers seat looked at the dash. Well this should be easy pulled the gear shift down to drive and took off. Pushed on the same peddle the policeman did and the car sped off. He put his foot on the brake and the car stopped so fast he almost went through the windshield.

I wont do that again he said. I had better hurry up before he wakes up he looked in the back seat and the policeman was still sleeping. The radio stared calling for the policeman. The wizard grabbed the call box and changed his voice to the policeman's voice this is car twenty two the person on the other side said they needed him back at the precinct right away.

Ok be there as soon as I can.

He started driving really slow down the road swerving for a while until he got used to the vehicle. When he found the road he was looking for he turned down it. Then checked the mail boxes and found Elphany's house. The wizard pushed on the brakes slowly this time. And pulled the vehicle to the side of the road.

His heart was racing when he saw her dancing in the big picture window. The way she danced was entrancing. She is still as beautiful as the first day I saw here dancing in the garden. Then it turned to anger when he seen the man that took her away grab her and held her close to him and started dancing with her.

I should kill the both of them now. He said in an angry voice.

But I will wait until they get back to Pholigue. The wizard looked in the back seat and the policeman was still sound asleep, put the vehicle in park got out and walked up the walkway to the front door. And rang the doorbell. Elphany came to the door and asked who is it. The wizard answered it's the police Mrs. Sherman, can I come in to talk?

Elphany hesitated for a moment and said that voice sounds familiar but shrugged it off. She opened the door slowly and let him in the wizard was standing there with his backed turned. Then turned around fast and stepped in with his head down. Closing the door with his foot. About that time Joe came in to see what was going on.

It's the police Elphany said. The wizard slowly pulled his head up. Elphany and Joe grabbed each other when they saw them. Yes let me see the both of you together. The ones that deceived me. The wizard said.

Elphany spoke up what are you doing here haven't you done enough to us and how did you find us?

I want you to leave now your powers are no good here.

I will leave as soon as I say what I have to say. The wizard answered. Your brother is dieing. So after he is gone I will have what is rightfully mine. So you both are invited to my wedding. In addition when I do I will destroy the both of you. Right about then they heard a noise and looked up to see where it was coming from.

There at the top of the stairs was a young boy. The wizard anger flared up even more and his face turned red. He started after the boy when Elphany yelled run Jahdson and hide. The boy started running so fast that he was through the kitchen and out the back door and out of site before the wizard even got to the kitchen. Elphany yelled you will never catch him. The wizard stopped smiled an evil smile and said yes he does have you in him doesn't he.

A lot more then you can imagine. She said. Then he reached in his pocket and pulled out an a picture and threw at them. This is going to be my new bride. He said.

Elphany caught the picture in mid air and looked at it, looked over at Joe and then back at the wizard.

I will destroy you before you think of having her. Elphany yelled at the wizard.

When we get back I will find her and with both of us together we will destroy your evil ways.

Nevis threw his head back and started laughing an evil laugh, then lowered his head. And looked at them with so much anger.

Within seconds Elphany grabbed the gun out of his holster and shot the wizard. Hitting him in the shoulder. The next one I wont miss. The wizard fell back hitting the door. He pulled it open and started running towards the vehicle. Elphany was right behind did a flip and was on the hood of the car pointing the gun at the wizard. Elphany yelled out you mess with the people that I love you are going to pay dearly. And shot at him again. This time in the leg.

The wizard struggled to get in the car. Started the car up and put it in reverse. Elphany did a flip off the car.

The wizard turned the car around and sped off yelling back I will be waiting to destroy all of you.

About that time the policeman started to wake up. What is going on looking down to see he had different clothes on. As the wizard was speeding off. The wizard said shut up, reached in his cape and grabbed some more dust. And said well lets just say they weren't to happy to see me and blew some more dust at the police officer. The police officer slumped over and fell back asleep.

The wizard made it back to the ship in no time at all. Got out of the vehicle, took off the policeman's uniform wincing in pain. Then grabbed some leaves and put them on his wounds went to the spaceship opened the hatch and went inside. Closing the hatch behind him. Walked over to the captains chair and sat down, buckled himself in. pushed the buttons on the panel in front of him. The spaceship started up and he set a course for Pholigue.

Then he fell back in the seat thinking how good it would be to own the whole universe smiling an evil smile then fell asleep.

A while later the spaceship landed on the opposite side of the palace. He opened the hatch and fell on the ground and passed out. One of the servants was hanging laundry when she saw him fall. she looked over and yelled I need help over here it's the master is hurt running over to help him.

Four of the knights came running out to the wizard. Two of the knights picked up the wizard and carried him into the palace. Took him to his room and laid him in the bed. They took his cape off when one of them saw blood on his cape. The night quickly tore off the rest of the wizard's clothes. Then yelled for the maid to come in the room.

When the maid come running in she put her hand over her mouth, gasped and asked what had happened

In a faint voice. One of the knight's said we don't know he was passed out on the ground. One of you go get the doctor and the rest of you go back to what you were doing.

Then told the maid to get some hot water and rags to clean the wizards wounds.

When the other knights left the room one of them said why should we. We would be better off if he was gone. The other knight said shut up he can hear you. You wouldn't want that on your conscious would you.

I guess not he answered. Then took off running to get the doctor.

The wizard woke up and saw the knight was standing over him and said it feels good to be home.

What were you doing to get hurt like this. The knight asked.

The wizard told the knight the whole story.

Is she really that afraid of you? The knight asked. Then he asked the wizard why he was so mean all the time. I was told that you were once a kind gentle man and you couldn't hurt anyone or anything.

And now you could care less what happens to anyone as long as you get what you want.

The wizard looked at the knight and said mind your own business and do as your told and you'll stay alive longer.

Look at my wounds the wizard told the knight. When he did he was amazed at what he saw. Whatever she hit you with it went clean through your leg. And the one on your shoulder, I can see a silver object in there.

Get your knife out and take it out. The wizard told him.

The knight did as he was told. The wizard screamed in pain when the knight took the object out of the wizard's shoulder.

What kind of object is this that would cause this much damage to a person? The knight asked.

That my sir knight is what they call a bullet and it came from a gun. The wizard answered. I will make you one as soon as I can get out of this bed.

I have known you for a little over ten years and yet you have not aged a bit why is that? The knight asked.

The wizard looked at the knight and said that my friend is my secret and I will die with it.

Just then the made came in with hot water and rags set them on the nightstand and started cleaning his wounds. The wizard grimaced in pain. And fell asleep.

CHAPTER 2

Meanwhile back on earth. Elphany was out looking for Jahdson thinking there has to be a way to get back to Pholigue without Nevis knowing when they are coming. We still have the spaceship hidden.

Luckily no one comes out to the woods since everyone thinks that the woods are haunted.

When Elphany and Joe landed the spaceship in Timber Creek.

The town's people swore up and down there were ghost coming up out of the graves by the woods.

Elphany finally found Jahdson and he had found the spaceship. He looked at his mother in surprise and asked. If she knew anything about this, and how long has this been here?

She told him everything that had happened and how they had gotten there.

Are we ever going to see Tarah again? He asked her.

I hope so I do so miss her very, very much. Then she pulled picture out of her pocket that Nevis had thrown at her. And showed it to Jahdson. This is your sister Tarah.

He looked at the picture and then back at his mother, she looks just like you mom.

How old would she be now. He asked. She is ten years older then you. And you my son look like your father and me. And you are getting more handsome everyday. And you are such a charmer, you are going to melt any girls heart when you get older. I should have told you all of this before, but I really didn't know how to come out and tell you everything. Can I see inside the spaceship? He asked jumping up and down in excitement.

Elphany nodded her head yes. I will show you the inside of it. However you must not tell anyone especially your best friend. Cause if the police find out they will put us in a laboratory and do all kinds of tests on us.

He promised her he wouldn't say a word. He was more curious of what was inside the spaceship then what she was telling him. Elphany walked around to the front part of the spaceship, moved all the limbs and brush away from said.

As the hatch came sliding up and disappeared. Now we need to wait for a little while I haven't been here since we landed on earth and there is going to be a stale odor coming out. She told him. About that time the air started pouring out, boy your right mom it sure does stink and held his nose to keep the smell out.

Jahdson started pacing back and forth he was getting impatient. Elphany stood there watching and started laughing you act just like your father when you want something.

Ok we can go in now. Elphany said. Jahdson didn't wait any time at all he took off running in the spaceship. With Elphany following him.

Wow mom! This is great looking all over running through the whole spaceship. I have always read about this in books and magazines. Watched it in television and seen it in movies but no I see that it is real.

Then looked over and seen a bunch of wires hanging loose and said no wonder we could never get home the master cylinder is gone.

You know mom I think I can make a cylinder that will fit in there, I just need to find parts for it. Then we can go home and help Tarah.

Elphany grabbed Jahdson, hugged him, kissed him on the cheek. Tears pouring out of her. And started crying that would be great if you could do that. Then we could get to Tarah.

Then we can stop Nevis before he can get to Tarah.

The power that our family has when is the strongest when the whole family is together and the only living soul that could take it away is god. Then she went on and told him about the powers that she had kept a secret from him for so long and how they worked.

Jahdson asked what kind of powers he had. She said that I don't know unless you try them out I know you have some of my talent as far as jumping into trees swinging off of tree limbs, running really fast for long distances without getting tired and stopping and a few other things. Like when your dancing and you body starts floating in air.

I know mom I see the way you do it and it is awesome how you do it and so beautiful.

Jahdson tried to blink nothing happened then he tried to wave his hands around and nothing happened, I guess they don't work here but you know I can hear things from a long ways away he said.

Yea maybe your powers don't work here on earth we will have to wait till we get to Pholigue to find out. Elphany said.

We had better head back. You know your dad he worries about where were at when we are gone to long. Especially after what happened earlier and you can start on the cylinder the sooner we leave the better. Elphany said.

I can start working on it as soon as we get back walking out of the spaceship. Jahdson said.

Not any more tonight Elphany said its starting to get dark and I need to get supper going. We need to eat I am starving. Anyway Nevis will be indisposed for some time after I shot him a few times. And we should be there before he can get out of bed the she pushed a red button and the hatch closed put the brush and limbs back in front of the spaceship.

Its to bad you didn't kill him. Jahdson said.

Elphany looked at Jahdson in a serious voice I do not want to ever hear that from you again once you kill someone you will never be the same and the powers that we have if we ever think of doing anything like that will be taken away from us. These powers are a gift from god and its been passed down from my family for as long as the universe stands so please don't ever think of ever taking any life of any kind. Tears were falling from her eyes for her son to even think of hurting anyone or anything like that.

I am sorry mom I will never ever say that again as he hugged her.

As they walked back to the house Elphany was telling Jahdson about how it was on Pholigue.

You see I am a princess there. It is such a beautiful place to live almost like the way I have our place looking. I made it that way cause your father was really homesick. So this helps him some. Elphany said.

Is that why dad spends a lot of time outside? Jahdson asked.

Yes and the house is almost like what we lived in but way smaller. Elphany answered. Then she said that there were no such thing as the weapons that we have here. Just sword's knife's and bows and arrows. But we never used our weapon's stop it by our powers and love. And with our powers we will live forever. that's the gift we get from god. Elphany said. So we are like angels aren't we? Jahdson asked.

Yes you might say that. Elphany answered. And the people that are close to our hearts will live a long life to. You have been born with that and that is why they call us prince's and princess's.

Then why can't Nevis leave thing the way they are? Jahdson asked.

Because in his eyes I betrayed him and he cannot forgive me for the hurt I have caused him that he blames me for. At one time he and I was to be husband and wife, but he was called off to war on a distant planet to save Pholigue. He was gone for so many years I and everyone else had thought he had died in the war.

When I met your father I was heartbroken thinking of Nevis every waken moment even when I slept I dreamt of him coming back to me. Your father was there for me everyday. Then after about a year of you father trying to get me to be with him. I fell in love with your father and we have been together ever since.

There is still part of me that loves Nevis with all my heart but I could never leave your father he has been there for me all these years.

But with the hatred that Nevis has now his heart has turned cold and bitter. And I could never even think of being a friend to him. He is a very devious man right now. And he feels numb. And will stop at nothing to get what he wants from anything and anyone. So do not ever fall into his trap or he will suck all your powers out of you and destroy your very soul. Elphany said. Then she told him about the jewelry and thr powers they held. Jahdson asked where the jewelry was.

Hopefully your uncle Remus had given them to Tarah. You see Nevis thinks that I was wearing them when he had banned and he thinks that they were destroyed but you cannot destroy them at all. However if he sees that Tarah has them he is going to be even madder, cause he will not be able to get close to her while she is wearing them. At least I hope not. Elphany said.

Me either just think of what a man like that could do to a planet like if he got a hold of Tarah. Especially with the evil that's on earth now. Jahdson said.

Yes I know. Elphany said. Then looked at Jahdson and asked him how he liked this planet earth.

This is the only home that I know and I really don't like the idea of leaving all my friend's behind.

But my family needs me more then ever now so I am going to stand with my family through all of this. No matter what happens. And I really want to meet my sister. I bet she is more beautiful then her picture. And anyway I can make new friends there I will have memories and pictures of all my friends. And I can always come back sometime. Jahdson said.

I would love for you to meet your sister and I am so sorry that the both of you couldn't grow up together. I have not seen her since she was five so I bet she is more beautiful now. And she was very beautiful then.

And you my son you are no ugly duckling yourself you have always been a handsome young boy just like your father. Then Elphany gave him a hug.

You know when the cop gets his uniform back he is going to be coming to ask a lot of questions and a lot of people in this town will be asking to. And I still have his gun.

Well at least you tried to get rid of Nevis. Jahdson said.

Yes but that is not the way I wanted to go about it I should have thought about it first. Elphany said. If only I could change his heart of stone. Then we would not have anything to fear. But there's nothing we can do now but to eat and get some rest. Elphany said.

As they walked in the house Elphany went in looking for Joe while Jahdson went up to take a shower.

Elphany found Joe sitting in his chair watching the evening news. The reporter was on there saying this is Peggy Lynn from KLGB news its eight p.m. July twenty fifth nineteen ninety four. Something big has change our quite little town earlier today, we have the police officer to explain what has happened. When the camera had moved to the police officer his uniform was stained with blood.

The police officer said when I picked up this stranger walking on a back road of Timber Creek asked him for some kind of identification that's when he reached in his pocket and pulled out some kind of powder and blew it at me. Then started walking over to where the spaceship was. Saying that this was the same thing that had happened ten years ago. When my partner had disappeared. Whoever or what ever took him and did this to me will be coming back and we all need to be prepared for the worse. The police officer showed fear in his eyes. This person or whatever he is very evil and we need to stop him when he comes back and be prepared that more might come with him.

How could no one trust a loyal and trusted police officer that has been on the police force for over thirty years? The reporter came back on now you mean to say there are aliens amongst us?

Yes and I am going to get down to the bottom of this and walked off. The policeman said.

The reporter came back on. We will keep you up to date on that is going on. This is Peggy Lynn from KLGB broadcasting life.

After that Joe stood up and shut the television. What are we going to do now if they if they find out we are the ones that landed here too ten years ago. They will lock us up or maybe worse.

Now Joe calm down their not sure if we are the ones that landed here. All they know is there is just on spaceship. However if they do try to you have to remember what we went through when we first got here. All the questions and now this. Jahdson came downstairs and heard them talking and looked at Elphany then at his dad. Joe was whit as a ghost and slumped down in his chair. Elphany ran to Joe and Joe said call the doctor I think my heart is giving out on me. Elphany grabbed the phone by the chair and dialed 911 an operator answered. Elphany said I need and ambulance and gave them the address she was shaking so bad she could hardly get a word out. Elphany drooped the phone and grabbed Joe.

You know I am going to die don't you and I know it to. Joe said. If only you wouldn't have taken off that jewelry. I'd be able to live forever please go help our daughter Tarah she needs you now more then ever. And I will always be there in your heart then he passed out.

Elphany started crying. You cant leave me Joe I need you so much I can't do this without you. He started breathing harder. Then he was gone.

Jahdson was sitting next to his mother looking at his father sobbing do something mom help him don't let him die on us.

I can't Elphany said then looked at Joe now you are at peace I will love you forever and ever. And pulled him closer to him. She looked up and saw the ambulance pull in the drive. Pushed Joe back in the chair and kissed him on the lips. Got up and started walking towards the door. Stopped when she saw the gun laying on the floor she Tossed the gun to Jahdson and told him to hide it. Then grabbed the rug to cover the blood on the floor.

Jahdson caught the gun and ran upstairs with it.

Elphany opened the front door and let them in. He is in there pointing to the family room. Three of them walked in one with the base phone, one with the medic supplies and on with the stretcher.

They went to Joe knelt down and checked for a pulse, and started c.p.r. they worked on him for what seemed a lifetime but there was nothing they could do Joe was gone I am so sorry for your loss Mrs. Sherman. Joe was a good man. We will take him to the hospital morgue and have an autopsy done. Mrs. Sherman. No you can't take him away I want him here with me. She was crying so hard she could hardly get the words out.

I am so sorry but it's the law. Okay then please no autopsy I know why he died he has had a bad heart for some time now. I don't want him cut open like an animal. She started crying even harder.

We will take him to the funeral home then and he told her which one it was and got in the drivers seat and drove off.

Do not worry my love we will be home soon. Then she shut the door yelled for Jahdson but he didn't hear her. He was in his room with the headphones on. Working on the master cylinder and was almost finished when she walked to see why he didn't answer he. When he finished he took off his headphones and turned around to see his mom staring at him.

She seen what he was doing. I know what you are thinking mom we are going to be able to help Tarah.

Elphany was still crying when he put his arms around her and hugged her. I miss him to, but you need to pull yourself together, so we can get out of here.

Yes I know I have to go get your father so we can get him home to Pholigue. If I can get him home in time. If not I shall die along side of him Elphany said.

Okay you get dad and I will go put this in the spaceship. Jahdson said.

Get some food an supplies together and get everything ready for us to go I will meet you at the spaceship. Elphany said. About that time the phone rang I will get the phone hurry up and Go. Elphany said.

Elphany went down to answer the phone and Jahdson did as she said.

Elphany picked up the phone and said hello. This is the funeral home calling we need to know what kind of arrangements you need to make. I will be there shortly to talk to you about it. Elphany said.

Thank you Mrs. Sherman I will see you soon. The funeral director answered.

Oh by the way you haven't touched him yet have you? She asked.

No he just arrived a few moments ago the funeral director thought it a little odd she asked him that.

Please don't do anything yet till I gat there I want to bring him some clothes to put on him. Then she hung up. She went back upstairs and seen that Jahdson was already packing things that he wanted to take he was really exited about seeing his sister and what was going to happen when he got there.

Elphany looked at what her son was packing is there anything that you didn't forget she smiled and hugged and kissed him. I will be back before you know it. And I am so proud of you for being so brave. Keep a watch out for me and Elphany left the room.

Jahdson looked in his backpack to see if he had packed the gun. It was wrapped in his jogging pants. Then put his backpack on his back.

When he finished he went downstairs and packed the food and water and other things to put on the spaceship went outside and loaded up his wagon tied it to the back of his bike and took off through the woods to the spaceship. He made it there in no time got off the bike and went to the spaceship opened the hatch and went inside with his bike and wagon and closed the hatch behind him, saying to himself I hope mom gets here soon. She is so proud of me but I am scared to death. I wish I could go back home and go to bed and wake up in the morning and see that it was all a dream. Yet he knew better mom needs my help, really bad and I am not going to let her down. Anyway I am really excited to be able to meet my sister. While he was thinking of what lay in store for him he was putting the master cylinder in and set it. When he did it clicked into place. Then stood back and looked at it. It was a perfect fit. I couldn't have done any better if I tried he said to himself. Then he went into the other rooms to put things away hurry up mom I don't like being here alone it gives me the creeps.

Meanwhile Elphany went into her room grabbed two suitcases out of the closet and put them on the bed opened both of them and started grabbing as many clothes as she could for her and Joe. Then went in the bathroom and grabbed all the things they needed from there. Ran downstairs and put the backs in the trunk of the car and took off towards the funeral home. When she arrived at the funeral home, parked the car in front of the home, got out and went inside seen that someone was at the desk and walked up to him, asked for the funeral director the man escorted her to the funeral director as she was talking to him she asked if she could see him one more time to say goodbye. Yes you may but I need to ask you a few questions first. We've known your husband well ad he was a very loyal employee at the mill. Are you going to be able to pay for the funeral or was there insurance. He asked. Elphany started crying I didn't think of that at the time. She reached in her purse and pulled out a pen and the checkbook tell me how much it is handed her a Kleenex that was on the table. Then handed her the paper of what it would cost. I am giving you a discount of what it would cost I am giving you a discount cause you and your husband has done a lot of work for me over the years. She wrote the check out and handed it to him. Can I see my husband now? She asked.

He led to the room where her husband was. Can you leave me alone with him please? I'd like to say goodbye to my husband. She asked.

The funeral director left and closed the door behind him. Elphany bent down and whispered in Joes ear don't worry my love we will be home soon, I just hope its not to late. Then walked over to the door and opened it, looked around and could hear the funeral director on the phone. She tiptoed down the hall where the funeral director was, and listened to him her hearing was sharper then the people on earth were she could hear from a long ways away.

She heard him ask a police officer that was on television earlier in the day. She went back to where Joe was in, picked him up as if he was light as a feather and went out the back entrance looked around and no one was there so she hurried to the car opened the back door and laid Joe down in the back seat. And covered him with a blanket. Shut the back door real slow so it wouldn't slam shut, then went to the drivers side and got in. started the car up and took off out of the parking lot. Looked in the rearview mirror, how handsome he is saying soon my love we will be home. And together forever.

She took off down the road and was halfway home when she heard a siren looked in the rearview mirror and seen it it was the police officer that was on the television earlier she sped up and made it home in no time flat pushed a button to open the trunk and got out of the car took Joe out of the back seat, went to the trunk and took the bags out and took off into the woods.

The police officer came pulling in the driveway right after Elphany took off into the woods. He walked up to the house and seen that the door was opened looked down and saw the blood on the floor seeping from under the rug. Pulling his gun from the holster he ran out, around the house and looked all around the back yard towards the woods. Then he spotted Elphany running down the path a thousand feet away.

He couldn't believe how fast she was going. He started thinking about what had happened ten years ago and how his partner and best friend disappeared. He really didn't want to go back into the woods but it was his duty and find out what had happened.

Everyone thought they had seen a spaceship land out here and scouted the area everyday from sun up till sun down but never found the spaceship or his friend anywhere.

So they finally gave up the search. I never gave up and I never will until I find the answer to what had happened back then. And I would still like to have my friend back. He was still chasing Elphany all of a sudden she turned left and disappeared deeper in the woods.

He turned left and looked around slowing his pace to a jog. Looking all around him. All of a sudden he saw the spaceship. Looking around it boy this thing is huge how could no one have seen this? He asked himself. Then he saw the hatch was closing as fast as he could he ran towards it and rolled into the spaceship before the hatch closed. Made it in before the hatch closed. Stood up looking around it was wide enough for three people to stand with it not being crowded and it was about twenty feet tall the walls and were grey in color and the floor by the wall had vents running all the way to the corridor. He started slowly walking to the corridor holding his pistol in his right hand not sure of what he was going to see at the other side.

Elphany was putting Joe in a chair and buckled him in so he wouldn't lean forward and fall out. And kissed him on the cheek, he looked so handsome and he seemed to be asleep. She brushed her hand across his cheek like she always did when he was upset about something. And her energy of her love would always calm him down. Sleep well my dear Elphany said looking at him with all the love she had in her heart. We will be back together soon.

The police officer walked in when Elphany was talking to Joe looking at her as if she was going crazy.

Jahdson was looking at his mom dad is gone mom you can't bringing dad along. Elphany looked at her son I am sorry son I should have told you this before but I didn't think you would understand. She said.

After all that you told me, you don't think I would understand. Jahdson said. You'll understand everything when we get home. Elphany had sensed that someone else was on the spaceship and sensed that they weren't in danger so she let it go for now, she didn't want to scare Jahdson anymore then what he was.

We need to get going so please sit down and buckle up so we can take off.

That police officer wasn't to far behind me so lets get out of here before . . . . about that time the police officer broke in gun in his and shaking he was really nervous. I think it's a little to late for that Mrs. Sherman. Now please tell me what is going on, pointing the gun at Elphany.

She turned around and saw that he had a gun pointing at her seeing that his hands were shaking, I sure wish that you wouldn't have come in here. Elphany said.

All I want to know is what is going on. I always thought it was a little odd how you and your husband showed up the way you did years ago. And now I have almost all the pieces together, and you killed my partner. Where did you hide him? His voice started getting deeper.

Elphany said he is probably where we are going to and my guess is he is with the man that put you to sleep.

You see we were banned to this planet by the man named Nevis he is a wizard and very evil.

The officer looked at her with a puzzled look on his face he wasn't sure if she wasn't telling the truth or not.

That man that banned us to this planet for the rest of our life little does he know that the part he took has been replaced. Now I have to get my husband back home so I can help him or he will die. We have seventy two hours to do this in and that's what I am going to do you or no one else will try and stop me.

And if you want your friend back you will put that gun away and sit down and buckle up.

You and your husband have been very loyal since you came into this town you have always been there when people needed you. And you've never lied to anyone. Now matter how tough it was for you. But I think your husbands dieing has clouded you mind. And if you come back with me, I can find you a good doctor. Before it gets worse the officer said.

I am going to advise you to put that gun away and sit down or I can sit you down which would you prefer? Elphany asked.

He started to cock his gun. I wouldn't fire that in here so put it away. If you fire it off in here it will pop your eardrums. Now sit down and buckle up we are wasting time. He finally put the gun away and sat down and buckled up.

Elphany and Jahdson did the same. Then she pushed a button on the arm of the chair.

The spaceship made funny whirring noise.

The officer was hoping that it wouldn't be able to take off. Finally it started running and lifted off the ground. Then came back down when she pushed the button again it came up this time it came up off the ground.

Boy mom I can see why you said to buckle up, that was a pretty bumpy ride.

Well you know son its been years since I've even been in this spaceship. Then she pushed another button and they started going up in the air. She started typing on the computer keyboard and set a course for Pholigue and the spaceship went backwards then forwards and took off.

Elphany unbuckled herself, stood up and walked over to Joe and checked on him. We will be home soon my dear brushing her hand across his cheek, looked over at Jahdson and the officer and said you can get up now its safe enough to walk around. And I know you are curious about the spaceship looking over to the officer.

Why yes I am I would like to walk around this is all a bit to much for me right now. He said. So he unbuckled himself and stood up. Why isn't anyone steering the spaceship? He asked.

Because it is set to a course that it can maneuver itself. So we won't get lost in deep space. Elphany answered him. Please call me Stan. The officer said.

Ok Stan. Elphany said with a smile. When he looked at her the smile on her face was so warm that he felt at ease and could not figure out why. But he knew deep down that as long as he stayed with them that he was safe.

Pholigue he said. I knew there were distant planets out there but I never imagined in my wildest dreams that I would be going to one.

Yes and it is a very beautiful place that we miss so much. There is no pollution, guns and the people there do not rob anyone because they grow their own food and what they can't grow is given to them. Everyone works together there. Or at least that the way it was before we left. I am not sure what we are going to see when we get back home. Elphany said.

He look around where he was and all around was windows on the wall all he could see out the window was blackness and stars and the stars were going by so fast that it looked like a rain shower. I can't believe I am doing this. It seems like I am in a dream. He said.

Well if your dreaming please wake me up cause if want to help you friend you are going to have to be ... ...d of Nevis. If you don't you could get us all killed. And the planet could be destroyed in the process. Elphany looked out the window. I think we had better sit down and buckle up we are going to be going through a time warp. After they sat down they felt a jolt and they rocked back and forth in their seats. The spaceship started going faster. And it seemed like just seconds had went by then slowed down. But this time something was different happened the spaceship started shaking. Let us pray we can get out of this alive and land on Pholigue in one piece. It will only take a few minutes to get there. And I don't have time to prep the spaceship so we might be in for a bumpy rode they held on to the arms of the chairs as tight as they could. The spaceship started rocking back and forth then slowed down to almost a halt.

Jahdson broke in and said I can't believe the stars there sure are a lot of them out there. After they went through the time warp. It seemed like seconds and they were through it. Jahdson looked out the window I can see a planet down there. Is that Pholigue? He asked.

Yes and it feels so good to be back home. I am so sorry that I brought you here I should have made you get out on earth its going to get dangerous here for a while. Elphany told him.

Well we are here so there is no turning back now. You know I didn't believe you at first but now I am beginning to understand everything. There is really life on other planets. Looking out the window he could see that Pholigue was so much different then earth and he felt at peace looking outside. I will help you any way that I can I have been through danger many times before so I can take whatever is thrown at me. And if Nevis tries to stop me I will kill him. Stan said.

Well there are other ways of stopping him then taking his life and I am glad you are going to help but we are going to need more then one person to help us and I think our coming home will do it. Elphany said.

I wish I was as strong as you, I saw you running with Joe and those suitcases. I couldn't believe. Stan said.

Well to me it wasn't heavy, and it is true I am very strong. My son here is and so is my daughter too. She told him.

Jahdson looked at his mother. Am I really? I know that I have been lifting weights and the other kids my age couldn't lift the weight that I could but I really never noticed until you said something.

Yes you are son. But your sister has more power then the both of us. And if she has the jewelry on she is more powerful then ever. Elphany said.

Is there anyone else that that has powers other then your family? Stan asked.

That I do not know but I have the feeling we are going to find out real soon. As soon as Nevis finds out we are back. She told Stan the whole story of why they had to leave Tarah here with her brother Remus. Then she told him how Nevis had banned them off the planet to earth. You see That is why this is very important that we had to get back home. If Nevis gets to Tarah first there is no telling g what he is capable of and the powers he could have. If I hadn't shot him he would have captured the spaceship by now with us in it so I know he is still laying in bed at his palace. There is no telling what he would do with you here and with Joe the way he is now.

Ok we need to sit back down and buckle up we are about to land. She said.

They all sat back down. Elphany pressed a button on the arm of the chair. The spaceship slowed down even more.

At that time the butler was walking around saying to himself what a beautiful day it is. He was walking around towards the garden, the gardener was in the garden weeding. Why yes it is. He replied.

All of a sudden they heard a whirring noise, looked up in the sky and saw that it was a spaceship no it can't be looking in the window of the spaceship as it came down. Their home their home the gardener dropped what he was doing and started running towards the palace. The butler was not far behind him. It's a miracle. I can't believe their home. The butler looked up one more time as the spaceship was coming closer. He seen Elphany sitting in master Joes chair, a boy and another man but he couldn't see Joe at all.

Oh my god something is wrong. The butler yelled.

He started running in the palace when the maid turned around from what she was doing and asked what the gardener was blabbing about.

Elphany is back. Butler said with excitement in his voice. Oh the maid said and turned back around and went back to work. All of a sudden she finally realized what the butler was saying. Elphany's back she said over and over again. And took off up the stairs after the butler.

The butler made it to the roof in no time flat. oh god please let there be nothing wrong with master Joe. But deep down inside of his stomach he knew it wasn't good. And something went horribly wrong. All the servants were there forming a line waiting impatiently. The butler walked over to a on the wall opened the panel and pushed a button as soon as he did the roof started opening up.

Elphany landed the spaceship inside the opening of the roof. Elphany, Jahdson and Stan unbuckled themselves. Then Elphany walked over to the hatch and opened it. Turned around and looked at Jahdson and Stan take four deep breathes and she did the same you see the air here is a lot different so it will take a little while for you two to adjust to it.

Then she went back unbuckled Joe, picked him up and carried him out Jahdson and Stan right behind her.

The butler went over to her first. Bowed to her and said welcome home princess.

Princess! Jahdson said in surprise.

Yes I am a princess his mom said. What happened to master Joe? The butler asked.

His heart gave out. Elphany said as she walked passed the servants. They were all crying as they bowed and curtsied to her.

The Elphany told the butler to go down to the cellar and get the bottle of potion that has a heart on it. I need it right away. I only have twenty four hours to get the potion down him or it will be to late.

She started walking down the stairs into the master bedroom with everyone following behind her. One of the servants turned down the covers and helped Elphany put Joe in the bed. The butler was back with the potion and handed it to Elphany asked him to help her so she poured the potion down Joes throat.

Jahdson and Stan stood there watching. Stan finally understood Elphany, she was such a beautiful woman through and through. And not like the women on earth most of them dint know what true love really was.

Elphany wasn't like that she cared about humanity and she just proved it with her husband.

Elphany poured half the bottle down Joe and watched to make sure all of it went down then looked at one of the maids can you show Jahdson and Stan to their rooms. So they can get some rest. She looked at them are you hungry? They both shook their heads yes. Take them down and give them something to eat and see if you can find some clothes for Stan. He didn't have time to bring anything with him and we don't want Nevis seeing you in that outfit.

Tarah woke up and jumped out of bed. She could feel something was not right that morning.

While she was getting dressed in the outfit her uncle had made her. She sat down on the bed and looked at the jewelry that her uncle had given her. Thought about the things he had said to her. How the jewelry worked. I just cannot believe all that was true. Tarah said to herself.

She jumped up I had better check on uncle Remus.

She ran downstairs as fast as she could. Ran over to her uncle but it was already too late he was gone. Tarah started crying. Oh uncle why did you have to die its no fair you never did any harm to anyone. All you did was take care of me.

I get those hunters if it's the last thing that I do. When I'm done with them, I'm going after Nevis. You just wait and see. Their going to pay for what they did to you uncle. She kissed her uncle on the cheek and hugged him goodbye. She got down on her knees and prayed dear god please give uncle Remus a special place up there with you and take good care of him amen.

Then she got up, went outside, and called all her animal friends together. She asked them to dig a grave for uncle Remus. Then went over to his favorite spot and started digging. Tarah went out to the shed and started building a box big enough so her uncle would be comfortable in.

After she was done she went into the cabin, found some blue satin material, took it out, and lined the box with it then she made a pillow with what material she bad left. Carried the box out to where the animals had dug the bole, put the box down beside the hole and looked at all her animal friends and started crying. Thank you for helping me I couldn't have done it by myself.

She went in the cabin and started washing her uncle. When she finished washing him she dressed him in his good outfit and carried bim out to the coffin. I hope you like it her this is your favorite spot. She laid bim in bis coffin and put the lid on it. Nailed it shut. Picked up the coffin and placed it in the hole and picked up a handful of dirt, said a prayer for him. Asked the animals to put the dirt back in the hole.

Tarah cursed Nevis and the hunters for the things that be did to them. She picked some flowers and put them on the grave. Then she walked back to the cabin thinking of all the things that her and her uncle had done. Going on long walks, hide and seek hunting for food. They would only kill the ones that were dying. He showed her how to clean fish.

Tarah walked in, took the dirty linen off her uncle's bed, and replaced them with clean ones. Washed out the dirty ones and hung them out to dry on the clothesline. Then she went in to the cabin and started fixing herself something to eat. She was hungry after the morning she had.

She had eggs, ham and bread. While she sat there eating, she kept looking over at her uncle's place. Wishing he was still there with her. When all of a sudden she felt something cold go down her back. She shivered a little bit. Turned around to se what it was and there was nothing there.

That's odd she said. I guess 1m just a little tired. She turned around to finish her breakfast and she almost fell out of her chair. There sitting in his chair was uncle Remus smoking his pipe.

Uncle Remus said why you poor child I didn't mean to startle you.

But Tarah stuttered you can't be hear your dead. Yes I know but you did wish for me to be here, and here I am. Uncle Remus said.

I guess I know that now Tarah said. I just came to tell you a few things It is almost time my dear your going to have to get ready and start your journey. Those men are coming back.

Yes I know and I will be waiting for them this time. Tarah said. Now child Remus said. You have to get things ready to go.

Tarah finished her breakfast and put her plate in her sink.

Now you need to pack enough food for at least three days on the way to your palace. And when you put on the cape I want you to leave it on at all times when you are traveling. Uncle Remus said. Why don't you want me to take it off? Tarah asked.

It will protect you when you are fighting. You can use it as a shield to protect yourself from weapons. Or anything else that can harm you. Uncle Remus answered Tarah.

Now don't forget the pouch. You can put it in the pocket of the cape. Uncle Remus said.

Tarah stood up, walked over to the closet, and took the cape out. Then walked over to her uncles bed and picked up the pouch. Then she walked back into the kitchen. And sat back down. She then looked for the pocket on the cape it was on the inside of the cape. She put the pouch in the pocket stood up and put the cape on.

I wish I could have lived to watch you go through this. That way I could have come along to help you. Uncle Remus said.

You will be there when I need you. All I have to do is wish for you and you will be there for me. Tarah said.

That is right and I will be there in an instant unless God asks me to be somewhere else. Uncle Remus said in a sad voice.

And it's not your fault if those men would not have beaten you like that you would still be alive. I wish you would have told me about my powers sooner then I could have saved you're live. And I will pay them back for what they did to you. Tarah told him.

Tarah you must think of why they are doing this, they are under a spell and you must break it. Now you need to get ready. It will take you three days to get to the palace.

Tarah stood up and started putting things into a bag. Then she grabbed a water container that bad a rope tied around it and filled it up with water.

Then uncle Remus spoke up hurry you must get going. I love you so much you are just like a daughter to me. And I wouldn't change it for anything in the whole universe.

There is going to be a big surprise waiting for you when you get to the palace.

What is it? Tarah asked her eyes were filled wit joy.

You are just going to have to wait. Uncle Remus said. Tarah walked over to the other closet and took the other outfit out. Folded it and put it in the bag. Then she asked her uncle bow long it would exactly take to get to the palace. When be didn't answer, she asked him again.

Tarah turned and he was gone. Just like be used to do when she was younger. Tarah started laughing. So this is how it's going to be now.

About that time, Succoth was at the door scratching. He was a beautiful tiger but instead of having black and orange marks on him there was blue and green. And his fur was so shiny that your eyes would water when you looked at him.

He would sneak up on you and grab you before you would even know he was there, The only one that could hear him was Tarah. She could bear things coming from a long distance. Tarah opened the door and let him in.

Tarah grabbed everything she was going to take took one last look around and said goodbye old house. Then she climbed in the closet where the suit was banging knocked on one of the panels three times. When she did a secret door opened. She went through and Succoth followed.

She closed the door part way. Stooped down and waited for the hunters to come in. She remembered all the times that the hunters would come in and beat uncle Remus. Tears fell from her eyes.

About five minutes went by and she heard horses coming up the lane. She started to stand up when the front door came flying. Tarah ducked back down. She watched as they ransacked the place

Where is that old man? The knight asked. He looked and seen that the bed was freshly made. The old man must have died. Then Tarah is bere somewhere. The knight said.

Yes and it was just recently. This pan is still warm. The hunter said. I wonder where she is at then. The knight said. There are times when I wish that Nevis wasn't so' mean. The bunter said.

He never used to be like this until Elphany married Joe. If only he would have listened to her, he would have understood.

But if we don't bring back Tarah, be will destroy us. The knight said. were a different way. The hunter said.

Oh there is. Tarah was saying silently to herself,

If only the old man wouldn't have tried to fight us. The knight said. And be put up a good one. Tarah said to herself.

She must be gone because there is food missing out of the kitchen. Let's go she cannot be too far. The knight said.

As they started out the door Tarah came out of the hiding spot. She reached in the bag and grabbed a handful of sleeping powder. She walked to the door and yelled hey.

As they both turned around, she blew the dust in their face. They both fell to the ground fast asleep. Well that wili give us eight hours head start. Tarah told Succoth.

Succoth was h the food bag and water jug in bis mouth. Tarah asked him if he was ready grabbing the bag from Succoth and he took off running.

Tarah started reading the map. It said to go south so that's the route she took. Tarah had never been this far away from home before.

She always stayed close to the cabin. She was really exited about getting out this far. They had walked about forty miles. She wasn't even getting tired. She always walked around the forest by the cabin for hours. Always finding something new to do. And she was excited and scared at the same time.

Tarah looked at Succoth, lets run for awhile I'm getting tired of walking.

They started running after about twenty miles Tarah said we've gone about sixty miles let's sit and rest for awhile.

She took out the water jug poured some in a dish for Succoth and drank some herself. Succoth took off into the forest. And Tarah sat there waiting for him to come back.

AU of a sudden, she beard a noise. She yelled for Succoth. When he came running back, she told him to go see who was following them.

When be came back, she asked him if it was the knight and the hunter. He shook his head no. So they ran and bid. Succoth was in the bushes and Tarah was up in the tree.

Boy this outfit Uncle Remus made is really nice no one can see me up here it blends in with the trees. About ten minutes went by and, no one was in sight. so Tarah was about ready to fall asleep, when all of a sudden she looked down from the tree and seen someone walk by.

It was a man he was about the same age as Tarah, maybe a little older. He was ruggedly handsome. Tarah could not keep her eyes off him.

Succoth came up to the tree, and looked up and made a little noise to get her attention. Tarah looked down and smiled. Sorry old friend. Tarah said. As she scaled down the tree.

She picked up the bag behind the tree. Started following the man. Thinking to herself this is the first time I have ever seen a man. Except for uncle Remus. He was an old man.

Tarah was watching the man walk, how nice be looked, he had big muscles and when he walked, he carried himself, as if he could hold his own.

I wonder if he can help me stop Nevis. She looked at Succoth. Then she thought about what her uncle had said.

To be very careful about the people you meet. Cause some of them could be with Nevis. Then she thought about the man that she was supposed to meet. along the way.

She was excited about meeting this man but she was afraid. She stopped and looked at Succoth, I have a great idea. You sneak up and pounce on him; I'll come running to help him.

Succoth took off running after him. With Tarah on his heels, Several yards behind him. When Succoth jumped and knocked him down. Tarah came running OK get off the man. She reached out her right hand for the man to help him up.

I am very sorry, I hope be did not hurt you. No he did not the man said. Giving Tarah an upset look. That isn't a real nice way of meeting someone.

I thought someone was following me. When he looked up at her. his anger went away. I am glad it was someone as beautiful as you. He said.

Thank you Tarah smiled at him. And you're not so bad either. And thank you, he said in return.

What is your name? Tarah asked.

He bowed to ber and said my name is sir Shavoth, and what may I ask is you name. He said. My name is Tarah. See told him.

So your the one who put those men to sleep back at the cabin. Remus wrote me a letter and said it was urgent that I come see him. But when I had it was too late. Shavoth said.

Yes he died late last night. He told me that someone was going to help me. Tarah said. Now I am glad I did come. You are so beautiful. Shavoth said.

Tarah started blushing. No one had ever told her that. Except her uncle.

Well we better get going before those men show up they will not stay sleeping forever. Tarah said. Well they will have a headache when they wake up I hit them in the head with my sword handle. When I saw that Remus was dead. Shavoth said.

Tarah smiled those men deserve more then that for what they did to uncle Remus.

The sun was starting to go down as Tarah looked at the sun I think we better make camp. Are you getting hungry? She asked while picking up firewood off the ground. why yes I am. Shavoth answered I have not eaten since yesterday.

Tarah pulled some meat potatoes and carrots out of a bag and put the on a stick then propped it over the fire. Then she pulled out two apples, and handed one to Shavoth and kept one for herself. This will hold you over until the food Is done I the cat going to eat to? Shavoth asked.

No Tarah said. Although be is my best friend he is still wild I have never tried nor wanted t change him. I like him just the way he is.

Do you take to all the animals the same way as the cat? Shavoth asked.

I get along with almost all of them; there is some out. there that can never let you go near them. Because of something that a human has done to them and they will kill you if you try to go near them. Tarah answered him.

About that time, Succoth came back well I guess he has already ate. Then Tarah starred down at the ground with a sad look on her face.

What is the matter? Shavoth asked.

Tarah put her hands over her face and started crying I miss my uncle so much. Tarah There was silence for about five.

Shavoth stood up, walked over and put his arms around Tarah. Tarah looked up at Shavoth and me how I shouldn't have broke down like that.

That 's okay when your uncle wrote me he had told me how close you and he were. If you didn't cry. I would think something was wrong with you. Shavoth said.

And, when was this that he had written to you? Tarah asked.

It was about a week ago. He told me that you, he was in terrible danger, and I should come right away so I came as fast as 1 could. Shavoth said.

I am glad you came. Tarah told Shavoth. You re the first person I've talked to except my uncle since my parents dropped me off at my uncles.

He bas forbidden me to talk to anyone. He gave me precautions, if you would have been someone else. Tarah said.

Weill am glad I am who I am. Shavoth said.

Shavoth went over to finish fixing supper. He looked over at Tarah and said why don't you lay down for a while and get some sleep I will wake you when it's done. Shavoth told Tarah,

Tarah didn't argue with him she was tired. She laid down on part of her cape and covered up withthe rest of it. She was asleep in no time.

Shavoth prepared the food and put it on the fire. Sat down and watched it. He looked over at Tarah who was sleeping peacefully. How beautiful she is he said to himself.

He was falling in love with her. This cannot be he said. I hardly even know her, He wanted to go over and lay down next to her but then he shrugged it off. I must wait until she feels the same for me as I do for her. Shavoth said.

I will protect you always. Even if I have to die for you Tarah. Then he thought of what Remus had Said, and bad long talks with them but he never made a commitment with any of them. There was one that be had some feelings for. But none like what he feels for Tarah.

He wanted to spend the rest of his life with her. How could this be he was saying to himself. I do not even know her but I feel as if I've known her forever. I just hope she will feel the same for me as I do for her.

He turned the food to see if it was done. A few more minutes. Shavoth said to himself.

He stood up to stretch, walked towards the road to see if anyone was coming. Succoth walked up to him. Shavoth looked down at him and asked him if he would go down the road to see if anyone was coming.

Succoth shook his head and started running down the road. He didn't trust Shavoth, he wouldn't have let Shavoth bold Tarah when she was crying. He knew that he was authentic and he was going to make sure he was going to stay like that or he would have to kill him.

Succoth took off running and in no time, he was gone.

Back at the cabin, the knight and bunter were waking up. They rubbed their eyes and bead the knight looked around for a few minutes. I thought I was in my bedroom for a minute there. The knight looked at the bunter and said. She got away again.

Set the cabin on fire the knight told the hunter. The bunter went into the cabin started a fire into the fireplace. Then he took a log out of the fire with the poker then placed it on the bed when the bed caught on fire be kicked it over towards the window. Instantly the curtain caught on fire. Then be went outside and told the knight that it was done.

The knight looked at the bunter and said let's get to Tarah's palace that bas to be where she's beading. If she gets there before we do, we'll never be able to stop her. And she might be able to destroy Nevis. The night was saying to himself I hope she does find a way to stop him. He is an evil man.

The knight was trying to remember what his past was like before ten years ago. But be couldn't remember anything. When be asked Nevis about it,. All Nevis would say was that they grew up together, they had been friends since childhood, and they've always been loyal friends. Deep down inside he felt that he didn't belong here.

With this hatred that Nevis bas built up inside of him. The knight wants to get as far away from Nevis as he can. All Nevis wants to do is destroy anything and anyone he sees.

He looked at the hunter and was going to ask him how he felt. But decided against it. The knight knew that the bunter would go back and tell Nevis everything and be would have been killed. The knight had to think of a way to help Tarah. So he could find out more about his past.

Meanwhile back at the camp, Shavoth cheeked the food and this time it was done. He woke Tarah up and told her it was time to eat.

I guess I was pretty tired wasn't I Tarah asked. I guess so you didn't move an inch the whole time you laid there. Shavoth gave Tarah a plate of food, then he made some for himself.

Very good Tarah said. She finished her plate and asked for more. They ate almost everything that was cooked.

Shavoth took the dishes, and walked over to the creek and rinsed them off. Washed his hands and face and Tarah walked over and did the same. She started drinking the water out of the creek.

I didn't realize how thirsty I was till now.

Succoth came running up. Someone is coming. Tarah said. We need to put the fire out. They started throwing dirt on the fire. It started smoldering. That's not going to work. So she wished the smoke to go away. And it disappeared.

Tarah looked at Shavoth, climb up in the tree right there. Pointing at the tree. Shavoth climbed up in the tree. And Tarah took a few steps back and took a full running jump did a flip into the tree. Shavoth looked at her amazed your going to have to show me that move.

It will be my pleasure. Tarah answered him.

They sat there being quite as a mouse for about ten minutes. Well I guess who ever it was must have turned off. Shavoth said.

I'D find out, Tarah answered him, she whistled for Succoth. They waited for him to come running but he didn't show up.

Tarah told Shavoth whoever it is they will be here soon.

About that time, they heard someone coming. It's the knight and the hunter. Tarah said I'm going to pay them back for what they did to uncle Remus.

Tarah took the bracelet off her ankle, stretched it out into a sword. And jumped out of the tree. When she saw that they had rode by.

No Shavoth said to Tarah but she wouldn't listen to him.

She snuck up behind the knight and yelled are you looking for someone?

The bunter yelled out it's her, it's Tarah! As the two of them swung around to see who was yelling. Now we really meet. Were taking you to see Nevis. The knight said.

You not taking me anywhere as she raised the sword towards them. If you want me, you're going to have to right me. Tarah said.

I don't want to fight you. The knight said. All I want to do is take you to Nevis.

Then I guess you will die the same way you killed uncle Remus. You beat a helpless old man to death. Tarah told them. 23. The knight drew his sword, while the bunter was sneaking around Tarah, Shavoth came up to the bunter, tapped him on the shoulder, and said I don't think it's very nice, two people on one.

Is that bow you beat Remus?

No it wasn't. Be was a helpless old man. And be deserved to die. Be had something that master Nevus wanted, and I'm the one that beat him. Oh yeah, about that time Shavoth slammed his fist into the hunter's cabin, how's that feel? The bunter reached out with a left upper cut and socked him right in the left eye then bit him in the right eye, then hit him in the nose and the mouth, then in the gut. In about five seconds it was all over, the hunter was in the ground, passed out.

"Well I guess you've heard the truth". The knight said and "I'm really sorry about your uncle, I never wanted him to get hurt. Nevis ordered it to be done, and if I would have stopped the bunter, Nevis would have killed us both.

Tarah was very angry you know what will happen if you are lying.

Yes said the knight and Deserve to die but I want to help you stop Nevis.

Why would you want to help after ten years of trying to capture me, you are finally going to give up. Tarah asked.

I know it sounds weird the knight said. But for some reason I feel I do not belong here. And if I do not I would like to go home. Nevis sent me to find you, if I do not bring you back this time be will destroy me. Be wants you Tarah so be can take your powers from you. And we have to stop him first. The knight said.

You can come with us but if find out if, it is a trick, I will kill you. I'm going to stop Nevis with or without anyone's help. I know you did not beat uncle Remus. Because I saw everything that had happened. Tarah said.

She turned around and looked down at the bunter. He was starting to wake up. He looked up at her and was trying to get up. When Tarah swung around and stabbed him in the stomach with her sword.

As she looked down at him, she said I hope you die slowly as my uncle died. She then wiped the sword off in the grass, pushed it back into a bracelet, and put it back on. Then she picked up the hunter with both hands, put him over her head and threw him over across the road.

The hunter was screaming oh god no. Be landed about fifty feet away.

They stood there and watched him lying there. Your nothing but an animal and you deserve everything that you get. Tarah said.

Then she started walking down the road with the knight and Shavoth following her. I'd remember not to make you angry. Shavoth said.

Tarah looked at Shavoth and smiled. Then she looked at the knight and said just remember this knight and lets hope you never betray me.

The knight just stood there starring at Tarah, He was too afraid to move or say anything.

Tarah walked over to the creek, bent down to get a drink and started crying. When she was done, she looked at Shavoth and the knight you two need a drink so we can get going. When they were done, they started walking; Tarah looked at the knight by the way what is your name.

The knight replied it is Robert princess Tarah. He took a bow.

Shavoth said no wonder your uncle said to keep a watch on you. As the looks of it, you need to watch over us. You are a very strong woman. I thought when I first saw you, that you were a meek, timid woman. Now I can see that you can take care of yourself.

They walked along the path for a while when Succoth came walking up he was ready to pounce on the knight when Tarah said no Succoth its okay. She looked at Robert I would advise you not to make any sudden movements.

Succoth came up to Robert and sniffed him. Robert just stood there until Succoth was sure that it was all right.

He is not the one that killed uncle Remus. I killed the hunter. Tarah said. Succoth shook his head no. What do you mean no? Tarah asked.

She looked at Shavoth and Robert. We must burry and get to the palace. Nevis is going to find out about me coming on my side.

After what I seen and what he can do I will protect you until the day that I die I have seen what he bas done. Robert said.

How good of manners are the both of you? Tarah asked.

Tarah took off with Shavoth and Robert right behind her, Succoth was way ahead of them all.

After running for a while Shavoth and Robert stopped trying to catch their breath. Tarah was Sitting on a large rock.

We thought we lost you. Shavoth said trying to catch his breath.

No you did not loose me you two are just too slow. Sit down both of you and take a break. Tarah said.

Robert popped up and said you know Nevis is going to send some more men after us. Yes Succoth went back to and see what's going on.

CHAPTER 3

Meanwhile the hunter made it back to Nevis; be was bolding his stomach as he went into Nevis's bedroom.

Nevis was asleep when he came in. What is it that you want it had better be good. Nevis said. The hunter collapsed on the floor by the foot of the bed.

Nevis jumped out of bed. Looked down at the hunter. Anger raged all through is body. Who did this to you? Looked around where is the knight?

The maid came running into the room. Go and get some of my men. Nevis snapped at her, The knights' been taken Hostage said the bunter grimacing in pain.

Master Tarah is very strong this is what she had done to me. Can you help me? The hunter asked. So Tarah is just like her mother. He looked down at the hunter, I told you not to come back here without her. The knight has probably turned against me. You are at no use to me now. Nevis said. As Nevis pointed a finger at the no, the hunter pleaded with him no master I have been a loyal servant to you.

You have not been loyal enough. You let her get away again. Nevis said. He pointed his right index finger at the bunter out came a bolt of lightning, the bunter turned into dust

The maid came in master the men are coming. Fine Nevis said. Clean this mess up. Pointing at the pile of dust

She looked down and was disgusted in what she saw. She went out to get the broom, swept it up in a jar, and took it down to Nevis's lab. Put a label on it and put it on the shelf with the other jars. Nevis was screaming at the knights', I want Tarah here within the end of the week.

He tried to climb out of bed but the pain was too much.

Hopefully a couple of more days and I will be good as new. There was six knights' standing there, this is what will happen to you if you do not bring her back to me. He pointed his finger at one of them and turned them into dust. Now go get her,

They all took off running. After about five miles of not talking afraid to say anything. They thought that Nevis could hear them.

One of the knights popped up and said Nevis is really going mad.

I know the one on the right said but if we do not do as be says he will do the same thing to us that be did to the other knight.

They walked up to the cabin, was about to go in when Remus's spirit came at them. One of the knight's runs away screaming I thought the old man was dead.

So did I, the other knight said.

Well I guess he is not they all said at the same time. They took off running down the road.

They went in the direction of Elphany's palace. I am never going back to that cabin on of the knights said, it is haunted. Neither are we the other knights said.

They started down the road towards Elphany's palace. That place is protected by something and I am not going back there for any reason one of the knights said.

Lets get going we do not have much time left to get Tarah and bring her back to Nevis. I surely do not want to die. Neither do we the others said.

They started down the road. What is this power that Nevis bas on us. I do not know but if we do not do as be says well you seen what be could do.

They all walked in silence. All of a sudden, right before their eyes Tarah appeared.

Well Tarah said you have a choice you can all turn around and go back or be killed.

One of the knights' threw his head back and started laughing by you and two weaklings. They all charged at once. Tarah let one often put up a good fight. She said hold on I am really getting tires of this and she stabbed him in the stomach. He fell to the ground. Tarah looked over and saw that both Robert and Shavoth were fighting two at a time so she went to help them out I don't think it's very fair two against one of them turned around and started fighting with her. Tarah was so fast he didn't have much of a chance with her.

He fell to the ground before he knew what hit bim . . .

Then Shavoth yelled out in pain, when Tarah looked around she saw Shavoth fall down grabbing his knees.

Now Tarah was angry she ran and leaped to the knight and before be could raise his sword at Shavoth, again she hit the knight in the head with her sword. The knight fell to the groundunconscious. Then she went over to Shavoth to see how bad he was burt.

Robert was still fighting with one of the knights. The other one was laying on the ground about ten feet away. The knight tried to stab bim in the stomach and bit his arm instead.

Next time I will aim for your beart, you are going to die for betraying master Nevis. The knight said. Nevis has gone mad and I stop him before it is to late. By this time, Robert was screaming. Tarah and Shavoth heard every word he had said.

The knight went to stab Robert in the stomach the second time, missed, and bit his leg.

Robert screamed out in pain are you blind? They started clanging swords together. Succoth came running and jumped the knight when he did the knight fell on the ground, when he did he fell on his sword.

Robert put his sword in his sheath and ran over to Tarah and Shavoth are you two ok? He asked.

I am fine Tarah said but Shavoth is hurt. Oh boy Robert said when he looked at the wound. He looked around to find some kind leaves to put on the wound then be ripped part of his shirt to tie the wound so it would stop bleeding.

Do you think you can walk Shavoth? Robert asked.

I can try. When he stood up the pain was so bad that he screamed out and passed out from the pain. Robert caught him before be hit the ground. I guess I am going to have to carry him. Robert said.

No I will carry him Tarah said she put one arm under his shoulder and the other under his legs. she picked bim up as if be was only a ten-pound baby.

Robert's eyes got big when he seen Tarah pick Shavoth up like that.

They walked about fifty miles when Tarah said we must check bis wounds. She put bim down on the ground.

Robert opened bis shirt and seen that the wound was bleeding again. Robert went to the creek, found a shell, filled it up with water and brought it back to wash the wound.

He felt Shavoth, s forehead, Looked at Tarah we must get him to the palace soon or he will not make it.

I am not going to loose anyone else. I will not let him die. Tarah picked Shavoth up and started running with him towards the palace, Robert grabbed the bag and started after ber. I need to cover his wound before he bleeds to death.

Tarah forgot all about putting the bandage back on. She put Shavoth down on the ground, looked at his wound and felt his forehead, Shavoth was starting to breathing in deep shallow breaths.

Tarah started crying why does it have to be all the people that I love. God I wish it had been the knight instead of Shavoth.

Robert started putting the bandage back on the wound. His eyes got real big and he had to take a second look. Well I'll tell you one thing Tarah your wish really came true.

Tarah looked at bim then at Shavoth she seen that where the wound was it was gone.

About five minutes went by and Shavoth woke up. He looked around, looked at his wound seen

Robert kneeling over bim and at Tarah, She was standing over by the tree.

Robert helped Shavoth get up and said I'm going to go clean my wound, walked over to the creek took off all bis clothes and jumped in the water. Ouch he yelled I didn't think it would hurt that bad. Shavoth walked up behind Tarah. Are you all right? He asked her.

Tarah stood there silent for a moment. Then she turned around and looked at Shavoth. Why does all this have to happen to me? There were tears in her eyes. What did I do. to deserve all this I didn't they were given to me, and people have been killed so one person can have what he wants.

Ask for these powers they were given to me and people are dying so on person can get what he wants.

Are you talking about Nevis? Shavoth asked.

Yes. Tarah said. She was still crying

What is it, what could be wrong? Shavoth asked.

I watched my uncle get beat so bad that he died from the beatings. Then there was you.

Before Tarah could say anything else, Shavoth wrapped his arms around Tarah and held her.

He held her so tight that she felt the heat from every part of his body flowing inside her. He looked into her eyes kiss her on the lips. She wanted to resist him but she couldn't. All she could do was let go of her emotions. She was in love for the first time in her life. She felt butterflies in her stomach. After what seemed lifetime be let go and looked at her,

Tarah you know I love you. Shavoth said.

All of a sudden Succoth came running jumping at Tarah.

Well Tarah started laughing. Something has excited him. I guess he wants me to look at

Succoth nudged Tarah's hand and motioned her to climb the tree. I guess he wants me to look at something. Tarah climbed the tree looked over towards the west oh my its so beautiful. That must be my palace.

What must be my palace? Shavoth asked. The palace is over to the west about a half a day away. She climbed down and was going to yell at Robert when she seen he was fighting on of the knights. We have to help him as Tarah took off running into the creek.

As she was at the bank of the creek she took off her ankle bracelet, stretched it out, and made a sword out of it. Shavoth was right behind her, when they got close enough she could hear Robert and the knight arguing.

Nevis is crazy cant you under stand that. Robert said.

No he is not he has always been good to me. The knight said.

Really, what do you think he will do to you when you go back without Tarah? Because I am not letting you take her. Robert said.

Before the knight knew what hit him. Succoth jumped him, when be did the knight lost bis balance, fell in the creek and bit bis bead on a rock. He went unconscious.

You did it again Succoth. Now I owe you twice for saving my life. Tarah was laughing at him. Well I guess he likes you As she looked at Robert, she started laughing even more.

Shavoth looked to see what Tarah was laughing about, and be started laughing too.

All right, what are you two laughing about? In between breath's Shavoth asked do not you feel a breeze.

As be looked down, he bad seen that be didn't have any clothes on. He looked at Tarah and Shavoth. Very funny his face-turned all red and he took off to get dressed.

Succoth got there before be did and grabbed his pants and took off running with them. OK the laughs over give me my pants back. Robert said.

Tarah put her ankle bracelet back on. Shavoth grabbed ber hand and they started walking, watching Robert chasing Succoth.

They were about ten minutes walking when Robert came up behind them swearing at the cat.

Tarah turned around, looked at Robert, and started laughing again. His pants were ripped to shreds. Robert got mad and started walking ahead of them.

Tarah and Shavoth were laughing so hard that they bad to bold their stomach.

Shavoth goes. Come on Robert if you think about it. It sunny. Anyway, if it were Tarah or I you would think it was funny.

Robert looked down at his pants then be started. laughing. Well if you think about it that way, I guess your right. But this is the only pair of pants I bave to wear.

I think that when we get to the palace they will have some that will fit you. Shavoth said. What do you mean when we get there? Robert asked.

The palace is very close at band. Shavoth said. Yes it is, and we. will be there before nightfall. So. let's get going. Tarah said.

You know we should have checked the knight to see if he was dead Shavoth said.

Well whether or no we are almost home. Right now you have a home as long as you both are my friends. Tarah said.

CHAPTER 4

Meanwhile the knight woke up. Rubbing his head where he was hit. Boy that really hurts. I have to go tell Nevis what has happened. As he was walking he thought of what he was going to tell Nevis. I need more men to help me.

He was the only one left alive out of all the rest of the men and he planned on staying alive. But would he when Nevis found out.

He made it back to the palace. When he went up to Nevis's bedroom, Nevis was sitting up in bed eating. When the knight came in.

The knight bowed down to Nevis. I am truly sorry master they are all dead except for me.

I even went back twice to try to capture Tarah. But both times I was stopped.

A big cat was helping Tarah. So was Robert. He said you were crazy and you were going to be destroyed. Then he fell on the floor and passed out.

Well I thought you were going to be a loyal friend to me. I was wrong about you too. I should have killed you back on earth where I found you. I will get you Robert you just wait and see. Nevis raised his fists in the air, when he did a bolt of lightning and a clap of thunder went through the room.

He started to get up out of bed but he was still too weak. He fell back in the bed. I will get you for this Elphany and you will wish that you had never left me. Then he called for the maid.

She came running in the room. Yes master. Take this tray down to the kitchen and then come back and pt this man to bed.

When you are done doing all that go get Lavasco. Get him here as before the sun goes down.

She picked up the tray and carried it down to the kitchen then she went in the linen closet and grabbed some bandages. Went back up to Nevis's room and helped the knight to his feet and helped him walk into the room next to Nevis's room. When she helped him bed she started taking his clothes off so she could wash his wounds.

The knight grabbed her hand. What are you doing? The knight asked.

I'm going to dress your wounds so they don't get infected. At that she went in the bathroom filled a basin full of warm water and brought it out and laid it on the nightstand. She started washing the knights wound he made a noise every time she touched one of his wounds.

When she was done she put the bandages on his wounds. I can't believe you not dead with all these wounds you have allover you.

When she was done she put the cover on the knight went and dumped the dirty water out and put the basin away. And checked on the knight. He was fast a sleep Tears welled up in her eyes. Why was all she could say? Then she went to get the gardener. When she found him. He was out trimming the hedges down the walk.

She told him what Nevis wanted.

The gardener looked at her. Does he want someone killed?

I don't know he just wants Lavasco here before the sun goes down.

The gardener took off towards Lavasco's cottage. He was there within a half—hour. The gardener pounded on the door.

Inside Lavasco was sitting at the table eating~ Who is there? Whoever it is it had better be good as he got up to open the door.

The gardener was standing at the door shaking his voice cracked when he told Lavasco that Nevis wanted him.

What does my brother want with me? Lavasco asked.

He just sent me after you that are all. The gardener said.

Lavasco walked out the door and slammed it closed. Lets go see what my brother wants.

The gardener looked up at Lavasco he was huge and tall. He scared a lot of people that did not know him. And he was strong enough to take a tree out of the ground roots and all.

It didn't take long for them to get to the palace. The gardener was out of breath from running to keep up with Lavasco.

Lavasco went into the palace and the gardener went back to trimming the hedges. Nevis could hear Lavasco come in the palace when he closed the door it echoed all through the palace.

Nevis smiled an evil smile. Now my dear Tarah you will be mine by the end of the week.

By the time Lavasco was at the top of the stairs Nevis said come in to my room. Lavasco walked in the bedroom looked at Nevis. Why are you laying in bed I thought nothing could hold you down? Lavasco asked.

Shut up Nevis said. The reason why I sent for you are because I want you to go after this woman for me and bring her back unharmed.

Who is this woman? Lavasco asked.

It is Elphany's daughter Tarah and I want her back by the end of the week.

And I warn you if you come back alone or betray me. I will kill you. Nevis said. And how are you going to do that? You can't get out of bed and I am much stronger then you. Lavasco asked.

Well watch this. Nevis said. He pointed at the lamp on the bedside table, a bolt of lightning, shot through is. At that the lamp was nothing but ashes.

Ok I believe you, but why don't you do it yourself? Lavasco asked.

Because as you can see. I'm stuck in this bed. I tried to get out several times I am still to weak. Nevis answered.

I know you won't betray me like all the rest of them have. That is why I sent for you. I have already sent seven men after her all of them died but two one came back half dead and the other betrayed me. I want the one that betrayed me brought back.

And if you have to kill him do so. Now go and get Tarah. Get some sleep first and leave at daybreak and take the knight that came back. And I warn you come back empty and I will kill you. Nevis said.

Lavasco stated to walk out of the room then he turned around and looked at Nevis. I shall do this for you only because you are my brother and even though you have a lot of hatred in your heart I still love you. At that Lavasco walked out of the room.

My brother, the ogre. Nevis said as he scooted down in the bed. I can't wait till Tarah is here then all my work will be complete. He rolled over and winced in pain and fell fast asleep.

When Lavasco woke up in the morning he went to take a bath. As he was washing he sat there asking himself why won't Nevis let me move back in? After all this is my home. He climbed out of the tub, dried off. And went to the closet to get some clothes that he had left. When he put them on. They had still fit him.

Well at least all my clothes still fit.

I am going to find a way to get my home back. Nevis has destroyed most of what my parents worked hard for. way is Nevis being so cruel? Lavasco asked. If only he would listen to Elphany she was so unhappy when she thought he was dead. And that was years ago.

They made such a beautiful couple. And the powers that Elphany had. Oh my god that is why he wants Tarah. We will see if he gets her here or not I never thought that he would be this desperate to get back at Elphany.

But I am going to make sure it doesn't happen.

I will take some of the knights with me and try to talk them into helping me. And if they refuse I will go into one of my fits and kill them all. I had better shut up before someone hears me. Lavasco said.

He finished dressing and went to check on Nevis. Well at least he's still

Sleeping. He went down to the kitchen. There the maid was fixing breakfast. he snuck up behind her and said well I guess your still here beautiful. Lavasco said.

The maid spun around startled. Lavasco she yelled as she put her arms around him and hugged him. Where have you all these years? I missed you so. The maid was so happy she was crying.

She let go and said sit down I will get you something to eat.

I will if you sit and eat with me.

She fixed two plates of food and as they ate they talked about old times. They forgot about what was going on. And for the first time in years the maid was laughing. When they were finished the maid picked up the plates and put them in the sink.

Why are you here? The maid asked.

Nevis sent for me. He wants me to go after Tarah. Lavasco answered. The maid was really hurt by the way Nevis was treating everyone.

Why can't things be like they were before Elphany showed up? Its all her fault that things are the way they are.

Now you can't blame the way Nevis is on Elphany. Lavasco said.

Lavasco grabbed the maid and held her in his arms. You are so beautiful if you would have married me when I asked you to you would not be a maid.

Yes I know but my heart is with another and it would not have been fair on you. The maid said.

And you still love him. Lavasco said. He is no good for you.

I know but I remember how Nevis used to he before Elphany came along. I remember how he used to help me with my chores and spend all the time he could with me. Now he is so mean to me.

So why don't you leave? Lavasco asked.

He threatened to turn me into powder if I don't do ask he asks. The maid answered.

Lavasco was getting angry. Do you mean that he makes you do things like sleep with him? Lavasco asked One time eighteen years ago. I told him I was with child. Well he hit me in the stomach and told me to get rid of it. I was alone and the baby came early. I hid the baby in a secret room so Nevis wouldn't find out. You should see him now he is such a handsome lad. He looks like you and Nevis. The maid said.

What is the boy's name? Lavasco asked.

His name is Shavoth. Elphany's brother sent for him to help Tarah. The maid said.

Then I must help them too. If Nevis asks I left before the sun came up. Lavasco said.

Does Nevis know about any of the hiding places? Lavasco asked.

No all he does is go down to his lab and back to his room. And all he says is that I'm going to get Elphany back for what she did. The maid answered. That's good because you might have t o hide in there if things get out of control. Lavasco said.

We are going to have to bring Nevis to his senses or he will destroy the whole universe. Lavasco said.

At that they turned around to see the knight stumbling into the kitchen. He was in bad shape.

Lavasco stood up and helped the knight sit down in the chair. I guess that leaves you out on coming with me. Lavasco said.

I have to go if I don't Nevis will kill me. The knight said.

No he won't let's put him in the secret room. Lavasco looked at the maid.

Lavasco helped the knight to his feet and followed the maid they walked behind the pantry and pushed one of boards on the sidewall.

At that the wall slid open. Lavasco took the knight in and laid him in the bed. Will you get him something for the pain? And check on him from time to time. Lavasco asked the maid.

The maid shook her heads yes.

The maid took a candle out of the nightstand and lit it. There are more in the drawer here when you need them.

The knight looked around the room. There were paintings on the wall of a little boy. It must be Nevis when he was younger. The knight thought.

I will go get you something to eat, more bandages, and something for the pain. The maid said as she left the room.

The knight looked at Lavasco. Are you still going after Tarah? Yes I am. Doe you know where they were going? Lavasco asked him.

They headed west towards Elphany's home. But I will warn you she has these powers and is very strong. The knight said.

Well I must be off then I will be back with Tarah before the end of the week. Lavasco said.

I sure wish I had gone with Robert. Then I wouldn't be in this shape. The knight said.

As Lavasco left he said don't worry things will change real soon.

The maid finished fixing the tray of food and went down to the lab and looked on the shelves found the pain medicine put some of it into a small vial. And put it back on the shelf the way it was.

Went back up to get the tray. Lavasco was standing there waiting for her. Well I'm off when I get back I want you to hide in the secret room.

I don't want you getting hurt. If Nevis asks the knight went with me and if I need more men I will send for them.

And don't slip and tell him anything. He might kill you. Lavasco said.

I've been prepared for this for a long time. My son learned how to fight from Remus. He is so strong and courageous. Unlike Nevis he had to learn wizardry before he could be strong and powerful. The maid said.

Take care of yourself. Lavasco *said* as he kissed her on the cheek.

The maid watched him walk out the door and climb on the horse and ride off.

She grabbed the tray of food and took it in for the knight. The knight was sound asleep.

She tapped him on the shoulder to wake him. When she did she scared him. He jumped and almost fell out of bed.

I'm sorry master please don't kill me. I just couldn't make it. The knight said. It's all right. It's me. The maid said.

The knight let out a big sigh. I'm so glad you weren't Nevis.

The maid helped the knight sit up so he could eat. And handed him the medicine. After you get done eating take a tablespoon of this it will ease the pain. The maid told the knight.

How long have you been here? The knight asked. Since, way before Nevis's parents died.

You could leave if you wanted to. The knight said.

If I did he would hunt me down. I already left once before. The maid said.

Yes but he's only using you. I've always wanted to tell you how I felt about you but was afraid to say anything. The knight reached out and grabbed the maid's hand. And kissed the back of he hand.

I will take you away from here and make an honest woman out of you if you would let me. The knight said.

I can't I just can't. The maid said.

She said I have to go and give Nevis his breakfast please don't come out of this room for any reason. Now eat so you can take the pain medicine. I have to give Nevis his breakfast.

Please listen to me. I will take you away from here and take care of you. I love you. The knight said.

I'm sorry the maid looked at the knight and walked out of the room without saying another word to him. She didn't want to tell him she was in love with Nevis.

She was in love with Nevis. And when I go and give myself to him I'm going to tell him.

She went into the kitchen and fixed breakfast for Nevis, put it on a tray and carried it up to him.

Before she could walk in the door he was ringing the bell. She walked in the room. Yes master.

I think you know what I want. Nevis said.

The maid sat the tray down on the nightstand. At that Nevis grabbed her arm so hard and pulled her down on the bed.

She thought to herself maybe I should go with the knight. All of a sudden she called out oh Nevis I love you.

Nevis ignored what she had said just climbed off of her when he was finished. As she climbed out of bed he grabbed her arm and said don't fall too much in love with me. You will be leaving as soon as Tarah gets here. I'm tired of seeing your face around here. Now leave me to eat alone.

She bit back the tears. Went over and handed him his tray of food. Is there anything else that you would like master?

Yes I would like to see Lavasco before he leaves.

I'm sorry master he has already left with the knight to get Tarah. The maid said.

Well he had better bring her back. I am sick and tired of waiting.

He took a few more bites out of his food. Take this tray away. Nevis said. As she grabbed the tray he reached out and grabbed her.

She thought for sure he knew that she was lying. She dropped the tray on the floor.

He grabbed her and tore her clothes off and forced himself on her.

When he was done he said. Their Elphany that's what I'm going to do to Tarah. As the maid, tried to get up out of bed. Nevis hit her right across the face. He had hit her so hard that both her eyes and nose started swelling.

You will leave when I tell you to. And he hit her across the face again. This time her head swung back and she almost passed out.

When he finished he threw her out of the bed.

And don't even think of leaving cause if you do I will kill you. Nevis told the maid.

She pulled herself up off the floor and put on what was left of her dress and left the room.

He is getting worse she said to herself. I thought this time he was going to kill me.

She went down to the kitchen put the dishes in the sink and started crying. Why is he like this to me? All I've ever done was love him. This is what I get out of it. Well this time I'm going to leave and you can't stop me. The maid said to herself.

Just then one of the knights walked in. this one was just as mean as Nevis if not worst.

He grabbed the maid by the arm. I guess you like to be roughed up don't you? The knight asked her.

No stop leave me alone. She tried to get away and he threw her across the room banging her head on the marble floor.

No she screamed as he came at her. He forced himself on her all the while she was screaming for him to stop.

I'll see you dead for this she screamed at the knight.

He got off of her and was fixing his pants when his son walked in

The boy was a little off in the head room his father hitting him in the head too much.

The knight looked at his son had seen that he was looking at the maids naked body.

The knight pushed the boy on her no she screamed so loud it echoed through the palace.

Before the boy could climb on top of the maid. She lifted up her leg and kicked him in the stomach. At that the boy went flying back into the counter. Hit his head and passed out.

Look what you did the knight yelled and went over and started hitting the maid. The maid started screaming, holding her hands up to stop the blows.

What is happening? Nevis yelled.

When no one answered. He rang the bell.

When the maid didn't show up. He climbed out of bed, grabbed his cane and slowly walked out of his room. Down the stairs towards were the screams were coming from.

Anger was raging in him when he seen what the knight was doing and done. Nevis looked over and seen the boy lying on the floor.

The knight hit the maid one more time and knocked her out cold. What are you doing? Nevis screamed at the knight.

The knight turned with a start. His face turned white with fear.

How dare you. You are going to pay dearly for what you have just done. Nevis screamed.

Nevis pointed his finger at the knight and said you want to be stupid then there you are. At that he turned the knight into a donkey.

Hit him with his cane and chased him outside. Then he looked at the boy. Well I guess you can join your father. And turned the boy into a donkey as well.

He went over to the maid and picked her up and carried her up to his room. It took all the strength he had to carry her up the stairs.

He laid her in the bed. Went in the bathroom and grabbed a wet washrag came back in the bedroom and cleaned her up.

The maid started waking up, she was in so much pain she started crying. She looked up at Nevis are you better? She asked.

No I am not. Nevis answered her. He had forgotten all about the hatred he had inside of him.

All he could think about was the maid and how cruel he was to her. He went into the bathroom and started running the bathwater.

If I thought about how I was treating her I would have never done it. He broke down and started crying.

All of s sudden there was a crash and a thud. He hurried up and shut the water off. And went into the bedroom.

The maid was lying on the floor the table was tipped over. What are you doing? He yelled at her.

I have to clean for when Tarah gets here. The maid answered. Well just forget about her for now.

He helped the maid up, and walked her in the bathroom.

He took off the rest of the clothes that she had on and helped her in the tub. The maid started screaming in pain. Oh it hurts so much. I can't stay in here. Ok give me a few minutes to get you a robe and I'll help you out.

I feel lightheaded the maid said. And she passed out.

Nevis came back in to see her sliding down in the water. He gently shook her to wake her. She didn't even blink so he picked her up out of the tub, put the robe around her and carried her to his bed.

After he put the covers over her he went down to the lab to get some of his pain medicine. He looked around noticed someone was in here. He shrugged it off and grabbed the medicine and some ointment. Then went back up to his room.

The maid was awake when he returned.

He helped her sit up and gave her some of the pain medicine. I have some ointment here for your wounds. Nevis said.

She laid back on the bed and let Nevis put the ointment on her sores. He sat down next to her on the bed to put the ointment on her.

She screamed out in pain when he put it on the open sores.

I'm getting really tired she said. Her breathing was raspy and was getting worse. When he looked at her chest he'd seen that it was bruised.

He put another pillow behind her head and her breathing started improving. Nevis sat there and watched her sleep. All the hatred he had inside of him was gone.

She opened her eyes and could see him looking at her with love in his eyes. There's something I need to tell you. There isn't much time left. The maid said. What do you mean? Your not going to die I wont let you. Nevis asked.

Do you remember when we made love the first time? The maid asked.

Yes I remember it well and I should have stayed with you instead of Elphany then none of this would have happened.

And I still am going to finish what I have set out to do. He started to get that evil look in his eyes again.

Then the maid started talking again. And all his attention went to her. All I have ever wanted was your love in return. The maid said.

I know and all I did was treat you bad. Nevis said.

And how many times has that knight attacked you? Nevis asked. It was after every time you were rough with me.

But this time it was worse, it was like he was a crazy man.

And he would threaten to tell you that were lovers if I was to say anything. The maid answered him.

Well you don't have to worry about him anymore. Nevis said. The maid tried to sit up but the pain was too much for her.

I hope you don't get angry with me. I just want to die knowing that you love me. Can I have a drink? The maid asked.

Nevis went in the bathroom and got some water as she asked.

Looked in the mirror at him self. How stupid could you be? You are such a fool all these years you were so cruel to this woman. All she did was love you.

Now it's to late to do anything about. Nevis held his head down in shame.

He went back into the bedroom and handed the maid the water.

The maid looked at Nevis. Oh how I love you. I wish I could go back in time. Maybe things would've been different. And you would have loved me. The maid said.

Nevis grabbed her hand and kissed the back of her hand. I was such an idiot we would have had children and if I would have let you. I would have found love. She looked at Nevis when he mentioned children. And turned away fast.

Ok out with it. Tell me what's going on. Nevis said.

Can you please call me Rosey? You used to call me that all the "time when we were younger, the maid asked.

I remember it was my hatred and wanting revenge on Elphany that made me forget everything. Nevis said

Do you remember about eighteen years ago I told you I was with child? And you hit me in the stomach to make me loose the child? The maid asked.

Yes I did. I did not want children and I still don't. Nevis answered.

Well the maid said I had a boy and he looks like you. And acts like you when you were his age.

I told you to get rid of the child. Nevis stood up he was getting angry with her. He raised his fist to hit her then. Why didn't you tell me you kept the child. If I you would you would have killed the child and I. The maid answered. And I would have to. Where is the boy and what is his name? Nevis asked

His name is Shavoth. And I do not know where he is now. A messenger came with a letter for him and he left. I have dreamed for this day for a long time and now we will not be able to spend the rest of our lives together. My time is almost up. The maid said.

Nevis looked at the maid he could see that she was getting weary. Try and get some sleep right now. He forgot all about his pain until he stood up. But it wasn't as bad as it was earlier.

He started walking towards the door. Then stopped and went back to her. He put his mouth to her ear. And whispered I will never let you go I love you.

Then he left the room.

Nevis went down to his lab, started mixing different potions together. It took him almost two hours but he finally made the medicine he needed. He took some for himself. And sat on the stool and waited.

After a few minutes well it's not going to work. As he went to throw the bottle across the room he started to get the shakes then he felt faint and fell to the floor.

Nevis woke up about an hour later feeling like a new person. He looked at his wounds and all he saw was scars.

It works Nevis yelled.

Then he grabbed the potion and went back up to his room.

The maid was fast asleep but her breathing was getting worse.

His arms and legs started hurting when he started walking towards the bathroom the pain eased up.

I have a son. Why didn't I notice the child was here all those years?

I shall find out where he was hiding in the morning right now I need to get someone to cook and clean till Rosey gets better.

He went down to where the gardener was.

I need someone to come cook and clean for me the maid has taken Ill. Nevis ordered.

The gardener bowed down to Nevis. Yes master I will go fetch someone right now. Thank you Nevis said.

The gardener was startled to hear Nevis say thank you that all he could say was your welcome.

And when you get back I have another job for you. I want you to be my butler. Nevis said.

The gardener bowed to Nevis. It would be my pleasure to serve you. At that the gardener took off to fetch another maid.

Nevis went back into the palace went up to his room, pulled the rocker over by the bed. He grabbed Rosey's hand and kissed it she was still sleeping he reached for the potion and gave her a teaspoon full.

The potion worked faster on her this time. Her breathing was getting normal. He started getting drowsy so he lay down in the bed next to her. Wrapped his arms around her and fell asleep.

He woke up with the sun going down over the trees. He went to ring for the maid. When he seen that she was lying next to him. Her breathing was better and he lifted the covers to check her wounds. They were almost healed.

She was still pale in color but she was getting better.

He went downstairs to see if the gardener had brought someone back. Sure enough the gardener was instructing her on what to do.

When they seen that he had walked in. the gardener told the girl that this is master Nevis and you will obey him.

Yes sir the girl said. She went to start supper for Nevis. Fix two plates and bring them to my room please. Nevis said.

Then he turned and went back up to his room. Look at Rosey she was starting to wake up.

Rosey looked up and saw that Nevis was standing over her watching her sleep. I must start supper as she tried to get out of bed.

No you stay right were you are you need to rest. I sent for someone to help take your place. Nevis said.

A sad look came on Rosey's face. I guess I am not wanted here anymore. I will pack my things and leave.

As she tried to get up out of bed Nevis came over to her and sat down next to her you are not leaving I want you to stay right here and get better.

And helped her back in the bed.

About then the new maid came in with two trays of food. Thank you Nevis said as he raised a hand for her to leave. Nevis helped Rosey sit up to eat.

And he joined her. While they ate they sat and talked about the things they had done together when they were young.

When they were done eating Rosey looked at Nevis I feel well enough to go in my room now. I would like to get some of my clothes and take a bath.

Nevis stood up. I'll help you get in the tub and go get your clothes for you.

He helped her out of bed and in the tub. Then he went into her room and grabbed some of her clothes. He went into her drawers and found some pictures of a young boy. This must be my son. What a handsome boy he is.

He took the picture with him. Along with the things she needed.

As he went in the bathroom he held the picture in front of her. Is this my son? Nevis asked.

Her eyes got really big. She was afraid he seen the pictures of Remus and Tarah. Yes this is your son. Rosey answered.

I wish I had gotten to know him. But I was so bent on getting back at Elphany for what she had done to me that I, didn't care who I hurt.

Nevis said to himself I am still going to get her back if it's the last thing that I do.

I am ready to get out now she told him. Nevis stood up and grabbed a towel for her. Handed it to her and left the bathroom.

When she came out. She could hardly walk so Nevis helped her into bed.

When Nevis went into take a bath she hurried up and went down to check on the knight when she went in the room he was gone.

She went outside and he was getting on a horse and taking off. She was a little relieved that he left.

She went into her room and grabbed all the rest of the pictures except all her sons and hid them.

Then she went back to Nevis's room and climbed in bed. About twenty minutes went by and he didn't come out: So she got up to check on him. He was sound asleep in the tub. Rosey walked over and gently shook him.

What do you want? Nevis screamed at her.

I am sorry you had fell asleep in the tub. Get out of here. He yelled at her again.

Rosey left closing the door. She walked out of his room and went down to her own room she put her clothes on and went out to do her work. She started crying as soon as I can I am leaving. Well at least I had one day that he was mine.

Nevis came out of the bathroom. I shouldn't have yelled at her like that. Now she left and thought I was the same person as before.

He rang the bell and she came in with a broom in her hand. She was holing her chest it was still sore.

What do you think your doing? Nevis yelled.

I am doing my chores. You told me to leave so I thought you didn't want me around. Rosey said.

You startled me when you woke me up. He went over to the nightstand and grabbed the pain medicine and took some then he handed to her you take some to.

Then he helped her get out of her clothes and get in bed.

The maid came in to take the tray away. Will you go into Rosey's room and bring all of her clothes in here.

Yes master the maid said. and took the trays away. Then she came back with Rosey's belongings. Nevis showed her where to put them.

Then he picked out a gown for Rosey to wear.

After the maid was done and left the room. Nevis helped Rosey into her gown. Then laid down beside her and wrapped his arms around her and they both fell fast asleep.

Nevis woke up about an hour later, looked at Rosey. She was still sound asleep.

He climbed out of bed trying not to wake her. And went over to the box of pictures that she had. I thought I had seen more then this. Nevis said to himself. Then shrugged it off.

He looked at all the pictures Rosey and the boy. Rosey was so beautiful with her long black hair.

He grabbed a picture of he had of himself when he was eighteen then looked at the one of the boy. We look so much alike, Nevis said to himself

He put the pictures back, and climbed back into bed, pulled Rosey close to him and kissed her on the cheek. And said I am sorry I should have listened to you years ago. I would have helped you raise our son. Instead of you having to raise him all by yourself.

Rosey opened her eyes and looked at him with such loving eyes.

Nevis gave her a passionate kiss on her lips, then looked into her eyes I love you Rosey.

It had to take something horrible like what that knight had done to you to make me realize how much I did need you. He said.

Oh Nevis! Do you really mean that? Rosey asked.

All my life I prayed that this day would come. But wait what about Elphany. Rosey asked.

Nevis looked at Rosey. She will get what's coming to her for betraying me and she will pay dearly. And I will stand by your side my love, Rosey said. She had forgotten all about Shavoth going to help Tarah.

Nevis looked at Rosey, you have never betrayed me have you?

No I haven't I swear I have always been loyal to you. Rosey answered.

He kissed her again. Then made love with such passion that it felt like it was the first time for both of them. Rosey started crying I love you so much Nevis. I would die for you.

And I love you to. He said I will never let anyone ever hurt you again. Can you please get some rest now. She snuggled up next to him. And fell fast asleep. For the first time in years she had felt save.

Nevis lay there awake for a long time thinking of Tarah and Elphany I am going to have to fight them to get what I want and I am going to get Robert for betraying me.

He kissed Rosey on the forehead and went to sleep. He was dreaming about when he and Elphany was together the day before he had left for the war. He was standing there holding her saying I will be back. I have to help my people. Elphany was crying please don't go I love you so much you are the only man that I ever felt so close to and I am afraid that you are going to get killed if you go.

Your love will keep me alive and I will think of you everyday until I return.

A man came up to them. It time to go Nevis.

Nevis looked at Elphany I have to go. And gave her a long kiss on the lips. Please don't Elphany was sobbing now I don't want you to leave me.

But Nevis walked away anyway. Then he though about coming back from the war and found Elphany in another mans arms.

He woke up furious. You are going to pay for what you did to me. He looked at Rosey hoping he didn't wake her up. Then looked out the window and seen that it was daylight out there.

Then looked back at Rosey wondering why she hadn't woke up yet.

He kissed her on the lips and she didn't move. Rosey, Rosey he kept saying.

HE shook her. Rosey pleas wake up. He checked her pulse and it was really faint then felt her forehead and she was really warm he tried to pick her up so she would wake up and nothing would happen. He whispered I love you in her ear and she still wouldn't move. What is wrong with you, why can't you wake up?

Come on Rosey you are scaring me. Please wake up I promise I will never leave you if you just wake up. Nevis got up out of bed and put his clothes on.

Went back over to Rosey and felt her pulse again and it was still weak then felt her forehead she was still warm.

Nevis picked up Rosey and carried her down to the lab. He laid her on the table and put a machine on her chest pushed a button and it started pushing her chest up and down. You are not going to die on me do you hear me. Nevis said.

She started moving around. What's going on? Rosey asked.

Your going to be just fine you almost died on me. Nevis answered as he took the machine off of her.

Rosey climbed off of the table I am really tired now. She said. They climbed the stairs hand in had back up to bed.

After they got back in bed. He looked at her don't ever scare me like that again.

I am really sorry. Rosey said. They both fell fast asleep.

Chapter 5

Tarah was thinking about the way her uncle had raised her. I think he *did* a great job.

Robert started yelling. This place is beautiful. He was looking at the garden. He started running towards the palace when all of a sudden he ran into something and it knocked him off *his* feet. What is that he said in a surprised voice?

It must be an invisible shield to keep Nevis and his knight out. Tarah said.

So how are we going to get in? Shavoth asked.

I guess we will have to walk around the place to see if there is an opening. Maybe someone is outside. Tarah answered. I think I know how to get in Tarah said.

But we will have to hold on to each other, hands. She whistled for Succoth. Oh god, don't yell for *him*. Robert said.

Succoth came up to Tarah. I need you to go and find a way through this invisible shield. Tarah said to him.

Succoth took off running. Lets *sit* and wait for him to come back. Tarah said. Robert sat down and fell asleep a few minutes later.

Twenty minutes went by. Well there you are. Tarah said to Succoth. All of a sudden he gave her a warning that someone was coming. Then Tarah remembered what her uncle said.

Ok everyone make a circle close your eyes and hold each others hands Succoth put his paw on top of theirs.

Tarah closed her eyes I wish we were inside the invisible wall. As soon as she said that they were on the other side of the wall.

You can open your eyes now. Tarah said.

How did this happen? Robert asked.

When he did he seen the person coming. I am glad we are in here because there is Lavasco coming into view.

He is a big man. Tarah said. Lets go as she started running towards the palace. Shavoth and Robert took off after her.

Lavasco tried yelling at them when he made the horse start running. But with the invisible wall up they couldn't hear him.

He knew about the invisible wall. I guess I am going to have to find a way to get in there

He climbed off his horse and walked over towards the wall started pounding on it with his fists.

Then he tried to pick it up. That still didn't work he started to walk around the wall to see if he could find a way in.

That's when the knight that had. left him back at the palace came running up. Lavasco wait the knight yelled

Lavasco turned around to see who it was.

The knight told Lavasco what had happened to Rosey and what Nevis did to the knight. How is Rosy doing Lavasco asked.

Before I left Nevis was taken her up to his room. And she wasn't doing very well. I took off so Nevis wouldn't think that I bad a part of it.

Nevis is crazy enough that if Rosey dies he win go off the deep end and there is no will be no stopping him:

Lavasco said.

We have to find a way to get through this invisible wall. Lavasco said.

The knight started walking around the wall when he seen Tarah, Shavoth and Robert and a big cat walking through a lane to the palace.

I see some people coming up the lane. He said. Is Shavoth with them? Lavasco asked.

Yes be is, why do you ask that. The knight asked.

He is Rosey and Nevis's son that's why I asked. Lavasco told him. What did you say? The knight asked. His mouth fell open

I wonder if Rosey told Nevis about the boy yet. I hope he never finds out. If he does he will kill the boy and Rosey. Lavasco said.

They both started walking around the wall. There has got to be a way to get in there. Lavasco said. Sure looks like its going to be a hard one to figure out. The knight told him.

Lavasco started moving up and down the wall to see if there was any kind of opening. When he was just about ready to give up be tripped over something, lost his balance and fell on the ground. Grabbing his foot and rubbing it.

Lavasco whistled at the knight to come over to where he was. The knight came running up to him. What happened? He asked.

I found something. Lavasco answered. And pointed to what he had tripped over.

The knight bent down to see what it was, swept the dirt off of it it's a round metal object and there is a lever of some kind. He pulled the lever as· hard as he could and door came open.

Its been a while since that has been opened. Lavasco said.

It sure was hard to open. The knight said looking at the door wondering what was down there. He looked at Lavasco are you still going to betray your brother?

Lavasco looked at the knight you know that Nevis is a very evil man and I have no choice but to try and stop him. If I he is going to destroy the whole universe so I have to proof to Tarah that I am on her side. And I will be right by your side. The knight told him.

Lavasco told the knight to go get the lantern off of the saddle. And started climbing down the ladder.

The knight came back with the lantern and lit it and went down after Lavasco. Closing the door behind him. Boy its really dark down there, band me the lantern. When he got 'the lantern he climbed down with the knight right behind him. They were almost off the ladder. Lavasco went to tell the knight to watch out for some of these boards on the ladder they are really loose.

They were almost off the ladder when the whole thing came out of the wall

Jump Lavasco yelled. As they both jumped off the ladder the ladder came crashing down on top of them and chips of wood splattered both of them. They covered their eyes with their hands.

Boy I am going to be pulling splinters out of my arms for weeks. That was close the knight said. Yea to close Lavasco answered him. What is your name? Lavasco asked.

My name is Tripper. When I was younger I used to fall over everything that was in sight. So I got this nickname. The knight answered.

All right lets get going Tripper, we need to find Tarah and help her. Lavasco said

And I want to make sure that there is nothing to stop us f along the way so keep your eyes peeled for anything unusual.

Ok tripper said. But I can almost imagine what kind of traps the Nevis has set for us. Tripper said. Me to and I am keeping my eyes opened down here it is creepy. Lavasco said.

They started walking forward whispering to each other when all of a. sudden Lavasco stopped suddenly. Tripper ran into him. Why did you stop? Tripper asked,

Take a look for yourself. Pointing ahead of him. Lavasco said.

When he look where Lavasco was pointing, there were three knights that Nevis had sent a while back. Their bodies were mutilated.

Who or what could of done a horrible thing? Tripper asked.

I really don't want to stay around to find out do you? Lavasco asked maybe whatever its isn't down here anymore. They have been dead quite a while now Lavasco said but be alert just in case, be quite I hearsomething.

Whatever it is it sounds pretty big. Tripper whispered. Maybe it sleeping it sounds like its snoring. And the smell is burning my eyes.

All of a sudden it came out of a four foot hole in the wall and it was huge its eyes were red like rubies it had a snout of a pig, ears like a rabbit, a tail of a rat it stomach was like an alligator and its tongue was like a snakes tongue and it has gray and black stripes down its back.

Trapper started gagging on the smell. When it came out of the hole it started running at them. Tripper grabbed his sword as the beast came at them.

Lavasco ran around the beast and grabbed it by the tail and the beast started squealing really loud stab him in the belly Lavasco yelled as he picked it up by its tail exposing the belly

When the knight did greenish black gooey stuff came out of the beast belly.

Then wit Lavasco still holding onto the tail he swung the beast around and it hit the wall with the wall starting to come down.

It sat there shaking its head for a minute then got up and started chasing them. Screeching as loud as it could.

I think all we did was make him more angry. Lavasco said as they were running. He grabbed his sword out of his belt when the best came at him he sliced him across the belly again this time· the gooey stuff came gushing out jumping out of the way so the gooey stuff wouldn't get to him and told Tripper to get out of the way it's a good thing he did the gooey stuff sprayed out it hit a rock and dissolved it.

Look out Tripper yelled as the beast reached out and sliced Lavasco with its long claws.

Tripper started stabbing the beast with his sword.

Lavasco didn't like pain and worse of all he couldn't stand the sight of blood. The beast came charging at Tripper. Lavasco yelled look out. Tripper jumped out of the way.

Lavasco started swinging his sword around at the beast. When the beast turned around and came at him he swung his sword at the beast's neck then kicked it as hard as he could and it fell with a thud.

Lets get out of here before. another one comes out somewhere. Look at your arm that beast did a number on you. Tripper said.

Tripper grabbed his bag and took some water and rags out. Lavasco help his arm out so tripper could clean the wounds. Then tied rag around Lavasco's arm.

Then Tripper took a drink and handed it to Lavasco.

Thank Lavasco said. I guess I did need your help after all. I owe you one. How are your wounds? They are still a little sore but not as bad as yours. They will heal.

You know I had better go in first. That way I can get a chance to talk to them. They know that you are with Nevis and they wont be pleased to see you at all. Lavasco said.

I know Tripper said I would be glad to wait but first lets get out of here the stink is starting to stay on us I really need to take a bath and throw these clothes away. You know I was very loyal to Nevis until he turned evil. He is so possessed by the hatred he has for Elphany he cant see the love that Rosey has for him. I would take care of her if she would let me she is so beautiful. And Shavoth to be his son if Nevis would of found out when she had him there is no telling what he would of done to the boy and Rosey.

Come to think about it that boy is more handsome then the father. Trapper said.

Yea I know Rosey is so loyal to Nevis and he treats her the way he does she has never stopped loving that man.

But I know that Shavoth hates him and doesn't want to even talk to his mom about him. He just walks out of the palace every time his mom mentions Nevis. It hurts Shavoth that he never got to have anything to do with Nevis. And takes off for a few days or even weeks at a time.

He is so tired of the things that Nevis is doing.

I never thought my dear sweet brother would turn into a monster like he is. You know when mother and father was still alive they had wrote on their will that I was to take over cause I was the older brother. And when Nevis came back from the war he was so bitter when he found out that Elphany was married to another man. He had banished me out of my own home. Mother and father had died before the war had ended and since he was my brother I loved him very much I didn't protest I just left. Lavasco said. But there is something we can do now. If we just sit around and do nothing all this beauty around us will wither and die. Tripper said.

They both went silent trying to find a way out and what they were going to say. Yes I know. Well I think we have hit a dead end. We might have to double back. Lavasco said.

Tarah, Robert Shavoth and Succoth made it to the garden. The gardener seen them coming and came running at them with a shovel in his hands. How did you get in here? He asked.

Well this is my house isn't it? Tarah asked.

This is Elphany and Joes home and you are trespassing. The gardener said. Are my parents here? Tarah asked.

The gardener looked at Tarah. Dropped his shovel on the ground and bowed to Tarah. I am so sorry we don't get many visitors since your mom and dad disappeared. that's alright at least we know that you are a faithful employee. Tarah said.

Tarah ran into the house all the way through the kitchen yelling mommy, daddy its Tarah.

Then ran all the way. up the stairs into her mom and dads room as soon as she ran into the house-she remembered where everything was and it was as if she was a child again.

Opened the bedroom door hoping she would find them there.

Elphany woke 'up startled. Tarah is that you? Is my-baby home?

Yes mommy its me. And ran over gave her mom a hug and kissed her on the cheek.

Oh Tarah my sweet little Tarah. We've missed you so much. Elphany said and started crying. Tarah is that you is my baby back home? Joe asked in a very weak voice.

Yes daddy its me. Tarah answered him. And I am here to stay I am never going to leave any of you again. Why are you so sick daddy? She asked. She went over and gave him a hug and a kiss on the cheek.

I am sorry your father had a heart attack. But he his getting a lot better. Elphany said.

I am so glad we are back together again. I just wish you weren't so sick. Tarah said.

Her father looked at her. Well lets go out to the garden then it is such a beautiful day that I don't want to stay up here anymore. Joe said.

Are you sure you are up to it? Elphany asked.

Yes I am fine and it is such a joyous day today. Joe said. Elphany looked at Tarah you made a wish didn't you?

Yes I wished for daddy not to be sick that's all. Tarah answered.

Well I guess Remus has taught you well, I see you are wearing my jewelry. Did your uncle show you how to use them? Elphany asked.

Yes and I love this one the most the one with the locket on it. And I have had to use them a few times. Would you like them back now? Tarah asked.

I was hoping you would but they are yours now and you will need them more then I will because Nevis-is after you not me. And if you keep them on and use them well it will save your life so do not ever take them off. Elphany told her.

Elphany looked at Tarah. Can you go outside and wait for us so we can get dressed? Tarah gave her father a hug, then walked around and gave her mom a hug.

All right. Tarah said. I need to go down and get my friends I sort of left them alone outside in the garden. She went down to the garden and the gardener said the maid came and got them so they could get cleaned up.

Well then I will go to my room and see if everything is still in there. Tarah said.

When she walked in there it smelled musty from being closed up for so long. She went and opened the drapes and pulled the window open.

I see this room hasn't been cleaned since I left. There was a lot of dust in the room. She went back and looked at all the stuff she had. You know I miss all of this am mommy and daddy. She started crying.

The maid came in with cleaning supplies, and bed linen. I am going to need some different clothes then what I have in here. Tarah said.

Yes miss Tarah the maid said. And welcome home.

Thank you Tarah said. And it's nice to be home.

Elphany and Joe were getting dressed I can't believe that Tarah is back home. Joe went over and wrapped his arms around Elphany. Our family is finally together. And Tarah is so beautiful.

Well I guess we had better go introduce our children. Elphany said.

There was a knock on the door one of the maids came in with a tray of food for the both of them.

I'm sorry, I forgot to tell you we are having lunch with the whole family outside on the patio. Make a big feast and take it out on the patio please. Elphany said.

I guess we had better go meet our guests. Joe said.

Any friends of Tarah are friends of ours. Elphany said.

They started walking down to the patio. It is so beautiful here but you know if Nevis tries to come after Tarah we will have to go back to earth. And he doesn't know that we are here yet. You know that don't you Joe? Elphany asked.

Yes Joe said. And when he finds out he his going to destroy us. And the whole planet. I am not looking forward to this at all. Elphany said. If I had died would you go back to Nevis? Joe asked.

No I don't know what I would do without you in my life. You are my life. Nevis is a very evil man and I would never go back to him. Elphany said.

Joe put his arms around Elphany you are my one true love and I will always stand by your side.

I can't wait till Tarah aat each wall. Lavasco grabbed Trippers arm and pointed there was another bnd Jahdson meet each other. Elphany said.

Yes that will be wonderful. And who are these guys she brought with her? Joe asked.

Lavasco could not understand it why does it stop right here? Maybe we have to go back and go a different way.

They started back and looked east standing over the one that was dead. They started moving backwards. When they backed into the wall.

Lavasco looked up and seen a ladder hanging down we have no choice we have to go up it. I really don't want to fight this beast.

Neither do I. Tripper said.

Lavasco started climbing the ladder. Tripper was right behind him. Lavasco lifted the door and a bunch of dirt fell in on them.

You better hurry the beast is coming. Tripper said.

Lavasco jumped out and grabbed Tripper by the arm and pulled him out. The beast clawed at Trippers leg. Tripper screamed in pain.

The beast started Climbing up the ladder. Lavasco took out his sword and cut the ladder. The beast went falling down with the ladder on top of it.

The beast stood back up trying to reach up to get out. Lavasco took his lantern opened it and poured some on the beast.

That made the beast even madder. It tried to jump up and grab Lavasco. Lavasco lit the lantern and threw it down on the beast.

The beast went up in flames. It started squealing and hissing. And then dropped on the ground and died.

I hope there is no more of those things around. Tripper said. I hope there is none left either. Lavasco said.

What was that noise? And how did you two get in here. The gardener came running over to them.

There were a couple of beasts down there that are dead now.

Well I am glad of the four people went down there and never came back up. The gardener said.

They are dead. The beast killed them. And there are six down there not four. Tripper said.

What are you doing here everyone said that Nevis killed you. The gardener said. Well I guess it isn't true cause I'm right here. ~ld this guy needs his wound fixed pointing at Trippers leg. Lavasco said.

And he needs his arm checked. Tripper said.

Is there anyway you can make sure there are no more beasts down there? If Nevis finds out he will he will have them kill a bunch of people. Lavasco said.

Ok but first lets get the two of you taken care of. The gardener said.

Wait till Joe and Elphany see that you are here they will be so happy to see you. The gardener said.

I am so glad they still are my friends. Lavasco said. Best friends and they will always be. The gardener said.

They walked in and the gardener took them into the kitchen told the maid to help them with their wounds. I will go get Joe and Elphany. The gardener said.

The gardener went out to the patio were Joe and Elphany were sitting.

You're more then welcome to join us. Elphany told the gardener.

Thank you very much. But there is something in the kitchen that you need to see. The gardener said.

Ok we will go if you go get ready for lunch. Elphany said. All right I will be back soon. The gardener said.

Joe and Elphany went into the kitchen to see what the gardener wanted. The maid was asking Lavasco how he and Tripper got the wounds.

When he told her she said I hope they didn't follow you out of that hole. I don't think they will follow anyone at all cause they are dead. Lavasco said. I am so glad the maid said my husband went down there and never came back.

He was a very brave man to go down there. Lavasco said.

When the maid finished with Lavasco she went over and tended to Trippers wounds. I bet you two are tired from fighting those beasts.

I will take you up so you can take a bath and rest for a while. The maid said. Lavasco grabbed some grapes out of the bowl and started eating them.

Joe and Elphany had walked in the kitchen to see what the gardener was talking about. Elphany screamed oh my god I thought you were dead. And ran over and hugged Lavasco.

Well hello friend Joe said giving Lavasco a hug. I am so glad to see the two of you. Lavasco said.

This is Tripper he was one of Nevis's knights until he found out that Nevis would kill him if he didn't do as he asked.

I guess Tarah gave him a good beating. He was in bed for a few days.

Well come on out to the patio so you can meet Tarah and Jahdson. Elphany said grabbing Joes arm and walking out to the patio.

Tarah was sitting out there waiting for her parents. When Lavasco and Tripper followed her parents out to the patio.

Tarah jumped up when she had seen them with her parents.

Wait a minute Tarah their on our side. Elphany told Tarah.

That's good Tarah *said* cause I don't feel like fighting anyone right now. About then Jahdson walked in on them.

Hey son Elphany said. Tarah this *is* your brother Jahdson. Hi Jahdson said. In a shy voice.

Hello little brother. Elphany said.

Well now our family is complete Elphany *said.*

Yes it is we have our home friends and the loyal staff that work for us. Joe said.

Shavoth and Robert walked in the patio and so did all the staff with the food there was enough food to feed everyone for a week.

I want everyone out here eating that includes all the staff too. Elphany said. Tarah and Jahdson took off for a walk each of them had a plate of food. Jahdson told Tarah about how earth was and Tarah told Jahdson about how she learned how to fight.

They walked back towards the patio. You know I am getting tired I think I am going to go to bed early tonight. Tarah said.

Elphany spoke up listen everyone I would like to say something. First of all I am really happy to be home second we must get prepared. Nevis is trying to take my daughter Tarah and I am going to do everything in my power to stop him.

So I am going to need everyone's help.

We are here to stand by you and help you no matter what. Lavasco said. Well I think Joe and I are off to bed. Joe was looking a little tired. Goodnight all and thank you for being there for Joe and me.

Goodnight Elphany everyone said. Tarah came up and gave her parents a hug and kisses and said I am so glad to be home.

And we are glad you are here. Elphany said.

Elphany and Joe went up to bed.

The staff started carrying all the food and dishes out to the kitchen. Well I am going to bed too. Tarah said.

They all retired early from the long trip that they took.

The next morning Elphany woke up and looked over at Joe. He was lying there sound asleep. She got out of bed and went to the window and seen that it was still early morning.

I wish that things would go back t normal around here. But with Nevis hating me so much it will never be the same again until he is destroyed.

She went into the bathroom and cleaned up, got dressed and went down stairs. Everyone was still sleeping.

So she went into the kitchen and fixed a pot of coffee.

When the coffee was done she poured herself a cup and walked out to the patio. Sat down in one of the chairs and took a deep breath. It feels so good to be home. But earth was a nice place to live and if things get so out of control here then we will have to go back.

And this time Tarah is going with me. I will never leave her again. Tarah came walking on the patio with a cup of coffee in her hand. Good morning mommy. Tarah said. And put her hand on her shoulder. Did you sleep well? Elphany asked

Yes I did to well it feels so good to be home. Tarah said.

I have dreamt of all of us being together again. I cried for almost two months after you left me at uncle Remus's. Then uncle Remus told me the night before he died why you really had to leave.

I didn't understand why I couldn't go with you and what I done to make you leave like that. But I know now the reason and I love you and daddy so much that this time I am going to protect you. Tarah said.

Well thank you Elphany said but I am going to have to fight along side of you. I should have done this in the first place. Elphany said.

It's such a beautiful morning out here. I want it to stay like this forever. Tarah said.

Yes but everyday its beautiful out here. Elphany told her. Joe walked in with Jahdson right behind him.

You two are up pretty early. Is any of the staff up yet? I am famished. Joe asked.

Well let's go see what we can find to fix for breakfast. Elphany said. Tarah went out to the kitchen with her.

The staff was just getting motivated. When Elphany and Tarah walked in. Good morning everyone. Elphany said.

Good morning Mrs. the staff said.

We need enough food for at least ten people if not more. Our guests are still here. Elphany said.

The staff went to work getting the meal prepared.

Can you bring some juice for my son and some coffee and extra cups out to the patio? Elphany asked the staff.

They all said yes. And started getting breakfast.

Everyone was up and out on the patio when Elphany and Tarah came back out to the patio.

Succoth came running on to the patio wanting Jahdson to go play with *him.* This *is* my pet Succoth. Tarah. Said.

Well hello everyone said. Except for Robert.

Tarah gave a little smile at Robert when she had seen his face. The staff walked out with trays of food.

Handed everyone their plates then left them to eat. Shavoth walked in and said hello everyone.

Tarah went over and gave him a kiss and a hug.

Elphany and Joe didn't say anything until he got a little closer to them.

Oh my god Elphany said and put her hand over her mouth. Then stood up and was ready to fight him. How did you get in here? She screamed.

Get out of my house now. Elphany ordered.

Wait mom this *is* Shavoth. Tarah said.

Elphany took a better look. I am truly sorry you look like your father.

Yes he is my father. But he doesn't know any thing about me. And I am here to help you not him. And I have never met him. My mother kept me hidden from him all my life. You see I want *him* dead just as bad as everyone in here. He hurts my mother all the time. Shavoth *said.*

So he was not faithful to me at all. All these years he made me feel guilty for falling *in* love with another man. And he was doing it himself. Elphany said.

If we all go together in a team we have a better chance of taken him down. Lavasco said.

They all looked at each other I think he is right. And I need to put my jewelry on so I can get my powers back. Elphany said.

Tarah started to take hers off. Elphany waved at her no leave yours on I have my own.

And rang the bell for the maid. When the maid came in Elphany whispered something to the maid.

The maid shook her head yes and went out of the room.

When she came back she was carrying a box and handed to Elphany.

When Elphany took them out they were almost all the same as what she had given to Tarah but there was more powers in hers.

Elphany put on her jewelry and said now we are going to take care of Nevis. We have twice the powers that he could ever have. Elphany said.

For the first time in years Elphany felt good about herself the guilt was off her shoulders and she could hold her shoulders up high again.

Robert and Stan were standing there staring at each other.

Stan said don't you remember me Robert we used to work together on patrol you have a wife and child at home. They are still waiting for your safe return home. Nevis has a spell on him. Elphany said.

With her jewelry on Elphany put her hands in the air and said remove this hold that Nevis has on Robert and everyone around him. Elphany said.

Robert looked at Stan. I am so glad to see you the last ten years are just a blur. Lets go home so I can see my family.

I'm sorry we can't we are not on earth we are on another planet. Stan said. Don't kid me you are always doing that to me. Robert said.

If you don't believe me ask everyone here. Stan said.

The staff came and took all the dishes away. Everyone was done eating.

Elphany and Joe got up. We are going for a walk. We will be back later. They were going to their secret spot. That only they knew about. Joe made it for him and Elphany to hide in when they wanted to be alone.

Tarah looked at Shavoth I hope our love will last forever. It will as he grabbed her and kissed her on the lips.

They started walking out towards the pond. Holding each other's hand. I feel like going for a swim. Shavoth said.

Ok Tarah said. And she started running for the pond. With Shavoth on her tail. They took off their clothes and jumped in.

Shavoth grabbed Tarah and held her in front of him. You are so beautiful inside and out. I want you with me forever. I will always love you as much as the first time I knew I was in love with you. Shavoth said.

And I will love you more tomorrow as I do today. There will be no walls in our love only true love. Tarah said.

Shavoth looked at Tarah will you be my wife. And be with me for the rest of our lives.

Tarah looked at Shavoth tears were falling. Yes I will marry you and never leave your side.

You have made me so happy. Shavoth said as he kissed her. when they were done swimming they went back up towards the palace. Joe and Elphany were sitting there talking to Lavasco.

We need to get everyone ready the time is coming. And it wont is long before Nevis finds out that I have betrayed him. Lavasco said.

Tarah and Shavoth walked up and said guess what? We are getting married.

That is great Elphany said. Joe stood up congratulations. I wouldn't want any other way. And hugged both Tarah and Shavoth.

Lavasco walked up and said I am glad to see that you two are happy and I wish you all the best.

Thank you Tarah said I want everyone here to be my family and best of all you will be staying here for a while.

I just wish we had time for a big wedding and invite everyone to see it. Elphany said.

That's ok mommy all we need is who is here right now. Elphany smiled you have a big heart Tarah just like me.

Lets go see what we can get together the wedding will be tonight. Tarah said. Elphany and Tarah went into the palace and told the maid what was going on. The maid took them up to Elphany's room.

I have your wedding dress in here madam and went in the closet and took it out. That is beautiful mommy. I would be honored to wear it. Tarah said.

Tarah tried it on and the maid did a few sewing needs and she was ready to get married.

Elphany fixed Tarah's hair when she was done Tarah looked in the mirror. You are so beautiful you will make a beautiful wife. Elphany said.

When they were done. Joe came in is my daughter ready to get married. Yes she is. Elphany said.

You look very handsome today sir. Elphany said.

I must get dressed myself. Elphany said. She went to the closet and changed into a dress.

The staff was downstairs making the dinner for the wedding. The cake looks great one of the maids told the cook.

When Tarah was ready they all walked down together. And walked into the parlor. There was Shavoth standing they're waiting for her.

When he turned to look he was amazed at her beauty and wanted her more then ever.

She walked up and stood next to him. Shavoth looked in Tarah's eyes. This is the day I've been waiting for all my life with the woman I love to stand by my side. I will love you with the last breath I have in my heart and from this day on I will love you more with each day that passes.

Tarah looked at Shavoth with tears of joy in her eyes. I will never fallout of love with you are my one and only and as each day goes by the love I have for you will grow stronger and stronger. We are as one now and will be as one until time runs out. They kissed each other with a long passionate kiss.

Joe and Elphany were standing there crying that was so beautiful.

Well you two are married now. Elphany said. She hugged them both.

Welcome to the family Shavoth you are one of us now. Joe said. He hugged both of them.

I wouldn't have it any other way. Shavoth said.

As they left parlor everyone was congratulating them on getting married. Mommy I would have liked uncle Remus to be here. Tarah said.

He is child look inside your heart. That's where he is. Elphany said. They went out and had dinner and drinks.

Tarah and Shavoth cut the cake. And made a mess out of each other.

After everyone was getting the party started Tarah and Shavoth snuck out of the room and went out towards the pond.

He had the gardener come out and fix a spot for them. There was champagne a blanket and some fruit sitting out there for them.

Oh how romantic. Tarah said.

I want tonight to be perfect for us. Shavoth said.

He grabbed her and kissed her passionately on the lips.

And gently laid her on the blanket. They made love for the first time. When they were done they held each other and was looking up at the stars.

I am going to build a house for you and I. And it's going to be filled with love and laughter. Shavoth said.

And I will bear your children a boy and a girl. Tarah said. They held each other looking at the stars. And fell asleep.

CHAPTER 6

Nevis was in the lab when the maid came knocking on the door. Yes what is it? I am busy. Nevis said.

I have a tray of food for you. Take it up to my room I would like to eat it with Rosey.

Yes sir the maid said as she left.

Nevis went up to his room where Rosey was sitting up in bed waiting for him to come in.

Well hello he said to Rosey I see you feeling a little better. Nevis said. Yes I am. I feel good enough to go back to work. Rosey said.

46.

Not anymore you are staying right here. We have a new maid to do your work as for now on your job is to take a break and rest. Nevis said.

They sat there in silence and ate looking at each other and smiling. Nevis looked at Rosey and could see that she was getting tired again.

Get some sleep my dear as he kissed her on the cheek I will be back to check on you later. Nevis said.

All Rosey could do was nod at him she was too tired to do anything else.

She fell fast asleep. He went out and told on of his knights to come with him. Nevis went out to the spaceship, pushed a button to open the door. Went in and shut the door. Buckled him in the chair. Started up the spaceship and took off. You had better sit down and buckle up Nevis told the knight.

The ship went up in the air and took off towards earth.

A few hours later he was on earth again. He put it down in the woods close to Elphany's home. And shut down the engines. Opened the door and stepped out. Pushed the button and closed the door. Ten he covered the ship with brush so no one could see it. The knight followed Nevis to the house.

Good it's dark out hopefully their Sleeping their going to be surprised when I walk in and take them by surprise. They will have to watch what I will do to their daughter.

Nevis stopped and looked around when he made it to the Clearing. Oh good the lights are all out in the house. Went up to the back door.

Nevis opened the door a little ways and peeked his head inside. No one was around. So he went inside. The knight was afraid of Nevis he waited for Nevis to go in the house and he took off running and hid on the other side of the house under a pile of brush.

Nevis went through every room. There was no sign of anyone in the house.

Now he was furious. Where are you? I will destroy you and everyone around you. Nevis yelled.

The knight could hear Nevis yelling. He was shaking so bad that he thought Nevis was going to hear him. The knight could hear Nevis yelling for him. Then he got up and ran in the house he was afraid to stay on this strange planet alone but even more afraid of Nevis.

Nevis climbed in the spaceship and took off. He circled the house and the woods where he thought the knight might be. That fool either got lost or took off on me. I will come back for him later. Nevis said.

He looked in the woods and could see where there had been another ship. He slammed his fists down on the arms of the chair. Well they got the ship running he said.

Now it will be easier to find them. He headed back to Pholigue.

When he landed he had seen that there was some knights watering their horses he went over and told them get my horse ready we are leaving to get Tarah.

And if you aren't ready by the time I get back out you both will die.

He walked in and went to check on Rosey she was still fast asleep.

He reached in his pocket and grabbed some of his potion out.

Went in the bathroom and put some water in a glass.

Went back into the bedroom. Rosey was just starting to wake up. Are you thirsty Nevis asked Rosey?

Yes I am. Rosey answered.

He hurried up and drank the water and went in the bathroom and got more this time he put the potion in the water and brought it out to her.

Here you go. Nevis said as he bent down and kissed her cheek.

Rosey took the water and drank it all down. Nevis sat down on the bed next to her. And held her hand. I love you Rosey. Nevis said.

And I love you to. Rosey told Nevis.

At that she fell fast asleep. Ok now she will be asleep for a couple of days. He kissed her forehead. and got up and went down to the kitchen.

Told the made to put enough food in a bag for three people that would last a week. He went down to the lab grabbed his cape and potions and went back up to the kitchen.

When she was done he told her to keep an eye on Rosey she is not to get up and do any work at all she needs her rest. And have this place spotless by the time I get back. Nevis said.

The maid nodded and Nevis went out tied the bag to the saddle, climbed on the horse and said let's go to the knights.

I hope Lavasco has caught up to Tarah and is bringing her back to me now. It's almost the end of the week. Nevis said.

They came up to Remus's cabin. Nevis put his hand up to stop. He climbed off of his horse and went inside. He looked around the room, tore out all the drawers and found a picture. Looked at it. It was a picture of Rosey, Remus and Shavoth. The boy was only four years old. What is going on here? Nevis asked.

He threw the picture across the room. Walked out. Climbed back on the horse burn the cabin now.

The knights did as he said. Nevis watched as the cabin went up in flames then took off towards Elphany's land.

A big gust of wind went by and put the fire out. Nevis didn't even notice the wind he was so angry.

Nevis rode the horse for a few hours and seen it was starting to get dark out. So he said we will camp here. And climbed off the horse.

On of the knights went and collected firewood and the other got the Camp ready. He put Nevis's tent by the tree and the other two tents close by.

Nevis pulled the bag out and said fix supper to the knight.

The knight took out three plates and gave Nevis's his. They sat there in silence for a while.

The knight that was collecting firewood came running back there is a beast out there.

I tried to fight it and it broke my sword in half.

The beast was coming into the camp. Nevis pointed his finger at the beast and it turned into powder.

Was that the only one out there? Nevis asked. That's the only one I seen the knight said. Ok now go get the firewood. Nevis said.

This time the knight came back with enough firewood for the night. He started a fire and threw some wood on it.

Then he sat down to eat. I need one of you to be alert tonight to see if anyone or anything shows up.

Nevis got up and walked in his tent laid down and went to sleep.

One of the knights motioned the other to follow him. When they were out of sight of the camp he said I think that Lavasco is on Elphany's side.

Well I am not going to tell Nevis are you? One knight said.

No I'm not I don't want to die. Neither do I. The other knight said.

You go ahead and get a few hours of sleep and I will come wake you up the other knight said.

Nevis woke up a few hours later. Went out of the tent the knight was putting wood on the fire. When he finished doing the he stood up and walked around the camp to make sure no one was around.

Nevis walked up to talk to him. You haven't seen any sign of Lavasco have you? Nevis asked.

No sir. The knight answered. It's allquite here.

Tarah woke up with a start what's wrong? Shavoth asked. I thought I heard something that's all. Tarah answered.

Shavoth got up and looked around. Nothing is out there he said. Okay but I would feel safer in the palace. Tarah said.

All right Shavoth said let's go inside.

They got dressed and walked into the house went up to Tarah's room.

Climbed in bed and fell fast asleep. Shavoth put his arms around Tarah and went to sleep.

In the morning Elphany and Joe were down having breakfast. When Tarah walked in. Elphany looked up. Where's your husband? Elphany asked.

He's getting dressed.

Tarah had a sad look in her eyes. What's the matter Elphany asked? I miss uncle Remus. Tarah answered.

I know so do I. Elphany said.

Mommy how does Shavoth know uncle Remus? Tarah asked. Remus is Shavoth's grandfather. Elphany said.

You mean that Shavoth is my cousin? Tarah asked.

No he isn't really my brother your granddad and Remus were best friends so I always treated him like a brother.

Shavoth walked in. hello he said.

Hi Elphany and Joe said.

Tarah stood up and gave him a hug and a kiss. They sat down and started eating.

So what is going on today? Asked Joe.

I thought I might go for a walk and check out the grounds. It's been a long time since I've walked these grounds. Joe said.

Well maybe I will go with you Shavoth said.

And Tarah and Elphany can sit here and talk.

That sounds great Joe said. They finished eating and took off.

As they walked outside I didn't want to say anything in there but Nevis is on his way here to get Tarah.

He doesn't know that you and Tarah are married now. When he finds out he will kill you. Joe said.

Not if I don't get to him first. I have wanted to get him for a long time for what he put my mother through. Shavoth said.

You will not have to fight him alone. We will all be there to stop him. Joe said.

With that they went on walking and Shavoth talking about what he went through when he was younger.

Life is so hard sometimes. Joe *said.*

Nevis and the knights were close to Elphany's when all of a sudden the horse ran into something reared back on its back legs and the knight fell off. Knocking himself unconscious.

What is going on? Nevis yelled he stopped his horse and got off he walked up to the wall and put his hand out to see what had stopped the knight.

Ok do you think this is going to stop me? Nevis asked.

He pointed his finger at the wall. And said be gone. Nothing happened. Find a way to get in there. Nevis yelled at the knight.

The knight was waking up. Get up and go find a way in there.

The one knight came back I found a way to get on the other side. Let's go Nevis said. And followed the knight.

The knights went down first. Then Nevis followed. Light a torch Nevis ordered when the knight did. Well that's what happened to those knights that I sent after Tarah.

There was a six foot hole in the wall to their left we are going that way Nevis said.

The knights were hesitant but Nevis said if you don't I will get you. The knights walked in first they went about fifty feet and stopped something is coming they said.

Nevis said move I will take care of this.

He went. in front of the knights Sure enough it was another one or those beasts.

Nevis pointed at it and it turned into dust. There you go now go on in when they reached the end of the passage. It was filled with eggs.

He pointed his finger at everyone of the eggs. And got rid of all of them. Then he looked at the knights go see if there is a way out of here.

They went inside the cave and walked around there's a place on the far side the knight pointed at a far wall.

Ok let's go Nevis said. And he followed them out.

They went about a hundred feet. Well there is a door right there. The knight said. He went to open the door. Help me here it seems to be stuck.

Both the knights pushed and pulled on the door but it would not budge.

Nevis said move I will get it.

He pointed at it and a spark shot out of his right index finger and the door fell to the floor.

There you go no move on. They started walking through a corridor it sloped upward. They were at the edge of the invisible wall when they came out. Well at least we made it inside the wall. Nevis said. Lets go on further.

They walked through a path towards the palace. Nevis was smiling all the way to the palace.

He sent one of the knights up to the palace to see where everyone was. Nevis said I am taking a little break. And he sat down on the ground.

When the knight came back he said everyone was in the palace. The only ones that were outside were the staff.

Let's go Nevis said as they walked towards the palace. When I tell you I want both of you to hide and when I whistled come out.

They came within fifty feet of the palace. Nevis said go and hide. The knight's took off and hid on either side of the courtyard.

Nevis slowly walked up to the palace. Now we will see what happens he said to himself.

Joe was out in the garden with Shavoth they were picking flowers for their wife's.

When their hands were full they took them in and handed them to their wife's

Oh thank you both Tarah and Elphany said.

They gave their husbands a hug and a kiss. Lavasco walked in beautiful flowers for two beautiful women.

Thank you Tarah said. Elphany smiled. Well let's all go for a walk to the pond and go swimming. Elphany said.

Lavasco went out to talk to the gardener. Did you set fire to the hole? Lavasco asked.

Yes I did. The gardener answered.

Well let's go ahead and block the hole anyway. Lavasco said. In case someone else finds a way to get in here.

That sounds good tome. The gardener said.

They looked around to see what they could find. The only things I see are those Statues the gardener pointed towards the right. But they are really heavy it took a lot of men to put that there. The gardener said.

Lavasco went over to the statue and picked it up. And carried it back over to the door. And sat it on it.

I hope no one else will lift that thing because it is really heavy. Lavasco said.

Lavasco was looking at the statue. Who are these people anyway? Lavasco asked. They are relatives of Elphany's this place has been here for over one thousand years.

They are beautiful people. Lavasco said standing there admiring them. Well I have to get back to work the gardener said. Then walked away.

Nevis was coming in closer when he looked around he seen Lavasco standing on one side of a statue. maybe he didn't betray after all no one else was around him. then he saw Robert and the other knight that he sent with him talking to another man. Nevis was really mad now. I will not be betrayed again he said.

He didn't see anyone else around. Well I wonder where everyone else is. Nevis was saying to himself.

Nevis heard someone coming so he ran and hid.

Lavas co looked around the courtyard and seen Nevis running behind a bush. Lavas co snuck in the house. Are Elphany and everyone still in here?

Yes they are upstairs changing the maid said. Take those men over there and hide them now. With no questions the maid went and instructed the men to do. They all took off and hid.

Lavas co made it up the stairs just in time to see all of them walk out of their rooms.

Well what is this? Elphany asked.

We have a problem. Nevis somehow got in and he's out in the courtyard. Lavas co said.

Well I see he is still just as clever as he has ever been. Elphany said. Well let's go I know of a place that we can hide for right now.

Where's Judson? Elphany asked.

I will go get him. Lavas co said. I think he is in the kitchen. Well I am not going anywhere until I get my son. Elphany said.

Lavas co ran down stairs sure enough there was Judson coming out of the kitchen. Lavas co motioned for the boy to come over to him.

Your mother is looking for you. Lavas co told him.

They went upstairs. Elphany was so glad Judson was all right. Let's go now. Lavas co said.

They made their way up another flight of stairs. There was a wall on the right side of the hallway Elphany tapped on the wall and it came open. She walked in lit a candle and said come on in everyone.

When they went in it was like it was another home built in the palace but smaller. Were stairs going up to four bedrooms and there was a kitchen living room and a bathroom downstairs.

I had the staff stock everything we needed in here.

The maid came in with the knight's ok we have to stay here for a while. Lavas co saw Nevis outside.

Elphany told the made to get the staff together and put them in the other apartment down the hall.

One of the knights said I'd go with her so she doesn't get hurt. I know what Nevis can do to people.

All right Elphany said but be careful I don't want to loose anyone at all. Tarah was looking around this is nice and roomy. What do you think Shavoth? Tarah turned around where is Shavoth?

No you don't think he went to confront Nevis do you? Elphany asked looking at everyone.

That's just what he has done. Robert said. He was telling me that he was going to kill Nevis for what he did to hid mother.

Well I guess hiding is out of the question let's go. Elphany said. Do you have you jewelry on Tara? Elphany asked.

Yes I do mommy. Tarah answered.

If he hurts Shavoth I will make him die a painful death. Tarah's said. Let's hope we get to him before he gets to Nevis.

As they made it to the bottom of the stairs. They heard Shavoth arguing with Nevis.

How could you hurt my mother that way Shavoth was yelling.

She got what she deserved and so will you. Nevis said. He pointed his finger at Shavoth.

Look out Shavoth Tarah yelled.

Shavoth moved just in time a streak of fire went right passed Shavoth and hit a bush. The bush turned into dust.

Nevis looked at Tarah. You will be my bride and this man will die. Nevis said

How can you kill your own son? Tarah asked.

That's easy I tried to do it once before and I will do it again. Nevis answered. He raised his finger to shoot at Shavoth again.

When Tarah reached for her necklace and shot at his hand. Nevis grabbed his hand. Looked at it he'd seen that the tip of his finger was gone. You're going to pay for that one. Nevis said.

Nevis started walking towards Tarah there was an evil look in his eyes. Oh no I am not Tarah said as she bent down, grabbed the ankle bracelet off stretched it out and turned it into a sword.

So I see Remus has taught you well. Nevis said.

Yes he did and he was a lot better person then you will ever be. And I am here to stop you from hurting anyone or anything else. You are a very evil person and you will not hurt anyone ever again. Tarah said.

You will be coming with me and you will be my wife. Nevis said. Elphany stepped in you are not taking my child anywhere.

And who is going to stop me? You. I think not you haven't practiced you powers in a long time. Nevis threw his head back and laughed.

When he looked at Elphany she had her sword pointed at his neck.

Nevis pushed the sword out of the way and picked Elphany up and threw her on the ground.

Tarah ran over to her mother. She was alive but was knocked out when she hit her head on a rock.

Tarah grabbed her sword and started running at Nevis. Nevis held his hand up in the air. Tarah stopped she was stuck there.

Shavoth caught Nevis off guard and gave him an uppercut in the right eye. Tarah got loose I will have to be more careful she thought to herself. Succoth came running he seen that Tarah was in trouble.

Shavoth was punching Nevis everywhere. Nevis was trying to push him off. Succoth came running and lunged at Nevis. Nevis fell to the ground.

Nevis reached in his bag and grabbed some powder out and threw it on Succoth. Succoth fell to the ground unconscious.

Nevis stood up and saw Lavasco coming at him. You will pay for betraying me brother. As he pointed his finger a ray shot out towards Lavasco.

Lavasco held his shield up and the ray hit the shield.

The knights that were with Nevis came in and started fighting Lavasco.

It didn't take long and the two knights were on the floor knocked unconscious. Elphany woke up with Joe holding her. Looked around saw everyone fighting.

She stood up and grabbed a sword off the wall. And took off after Nevis.

Nevis seen Elphany and Joe together and that made him even madder he started pointing at anything and everything and turning it to dust.

Lavasco was walking towards Nevis.

The knights woke up and grabbed their swords.

One came running up to Elphany and grabbed her from behind.

Joe grabbed the other sword and told the knight to let his wife go.

When the knight did Elphany hit him in the head with the end of the sword.

Nevis looked over and saw Jahdson standing by the door watching everyone fight he went up behind the boy and put his hand over his mouth and took him hostage. Nevis snuck away without anyone knowing he was gone.

Nevis made it to the end of the courtyard with the boy.

Jahdson wiggled out of Nevis's hands and started yelling for someone to help. Shut up no one can here you.

Nevis grabbed the boy by the arm and dragged him down in the hole when they got. to the bottom. Nevis raised his hand in the air and sealed the hole so no one could get in and follow him.

Then he let go of Jahdson. Nevis looked at him you can yell all you want no one can hear you. Anyway there is a beast down here so if you don't shut up I will let it eat you.

Jahdson looked around and seen all the broken eggs on the ground. I am not the one you wanted so why did you take me? Jahdson asked. You are going to bring them to me. Nevis answered him.

Now lets go. Nevis said.

You are not my father so don't tell me what to do. Jahdson snapped.

Nevis grabbed Jahdson by the back of the hair and looked at him you will listen to me or I will kill you. Nevis said.

Ok let go of my hair. Jahdson said.

Shavoth heard someone yell for help and looked around.

The knights that came with Nevis were knocked out on the ground. Elphany told the gardener to tie them up.

The gardener grabbed some rope and tied them to some posts opposite each other. Then she told the gardener to get everyone together and bring them down here. Where is Nevis? Tarah asked.

Everyone looked around. He was gone.

Where's Jahdson? Elphany asked.

When all the staff was down there was no sign of Jahdson or Nevis around. Oh no Nevis took Jahdson. Elphany started crying.

How did Nevis get in anyway.

The same way I did. Lavasco answered. There is no way he could have came in the same way that I did. Lavasco said.

As he pointed at the statue.

Well there must be another way in. Joe said.

The gardener ran up to the roof. Grabbed a telescope and looked out over the invisible wall. There was Nevis getting on his horse and taking off. with Jahdson tied on another horse.

The gardener went back down and told Elphany what he saw. I'm going after him. Elphany said.

Open up the invisible wall. Elphany yelled as she went to get her horse. Joe and

Tarah right behind her. Shavoth was already in the barn had three of the horses saddled and one more almost done.

Lavasco moved the statue and went down the hole wait for me Tripper yelled.

There was no sign of the beast any where around so they ran to the end of the hole.

When Lavasco reached the ladder Nevis and Jahdson was already gone. Let's go Lavasco said. He started climbing the ladder. They reached the top. Elphany, Joe and Tarah were riding bye.

Lavasco whistled for his horse. Both the horses came running.

Lavasco and tripper took off on the horses and started off after Elphany.

Nevis was running the horses hard. I guess we are far enough ahead of them so he slowed the horses down.

All of a sudden the horse reared back and Nevis fell off.

Help me child he said.

Jahdson got off the horse pretended like he was walking up to Nevis. And turned around and took off running.

Get back here Nevis yelled. Jahdson kept on running.

He looked back and didn't see Nevis coming so he ran into the forest and climbed a tree hid under the leaves.

Nevis stood up and got back on his horse grabbed the other horse by the reins and set off to look for Jahdson.

Where are you boy I don't have time for this you had better come out or else. Nevis yelled.

Jahdson watched Nevis go up the trail. He stayed in the tree watching Nevis disappear down the road.

Nevis hurried up and got to the palace then he thought that boy couldn't have gotten this far.

He turned around and went back a little ways.

He gave up and turned the horse around and went home. I will find you boy and when I do you will be sorry you ever took off on me. Nevis screamed.

Nevis was really mad I am going to destroy everyone of you do you hear me Elphany? Nevis yelled.

Jahdson sat in the tree for a long time afraid to move hurry mom and dad. I want to go back home. I don't like it here. That man is an evil man.

Lavasco and Tripper finally caught up with Elphany and the rest.

Well there no in the hole. Lavasco said.

Well we must hurry Elphany said.

I am going to go through the woods to see if they were hiding in there. Lavasco went into the trees and looked around.

How far would they have gone? Succoth went with Lavasco. Jahdson looked down and seen Succoth standing under the tree.

Hey buddy Jahdson said. Succoth looked up and Jahdson climbed down from the tree.

Here I am Jahdson yelled. Lavasco turned around and looked. I am so glad you got away. Lavasco said. Climb up on the horse. Lavasco told Jahdson.

When Jahdson did. Lavasco took off to get Elphany.

Hey everyone guess who I found Lavasco yelled out.

Elphany turned the horse around and trotted back to get Jahdson. I am so glad you are all right. Elphany said grabbing Jahdson and hugging him. Joe was right behind her. Climb on my horse son.

And we will ride home. Let's go home Elphany said.

We will catch up Tarah said as she looked at Shavoth. We want to ride around. And I think Nevis went home for now. He won't be back for a while. Tarah said. Ok Elphany sad I will see you at home later.

Tarah and Shavoth went towards the north I want to find some land for us to live on Tarah said.

Nevis was watching everything. Now is my chance. He rode up behind Tarah and Shavoth in a slow pace.

He reached in his cape and pulled out a small leather bag.

He reached in and grabbed a hand full of blue colored powder. And rode up next to both Tarah and Shavoth.

When Tarah and Shavoth looked over he blew at both of them. Both Tarah and Shavoth fell to the ground unconscious.

Nevis climbed off his horse and scooped Tarah up in his arms and threw her on the horse.

And took off towards the palace. You fools did you think you could stop me. Nevis yelled as he pulled the reins back and the horse took off running. Elphany was so happy that Nevis didn't get the chance to hurt Jahdson. Let's take a little break Elphany said.

They all climbed off the horses and let the horses drink from the creek. Shavoth woke up looked around dazed. Tarah are you all right. There was no sign of her or her horse.

No you can't have my wife Shavoth yelled I would save you Tarah.

Shavoth climbed on his horse and took off to find Elphany and the others.

They weren't far away as he came riding up.

He didn't even get off the horse just yelled Nevis has Tarah. Elphany looked at Joe and the rest of them.

Succoth and Jahdson were playing.

54.

Elphany looked at Succoth get Jahdson home. And bring back as many people as you can.

Succoth looked and seen Elphany was on her horse and nodded.

Elphany and the rest climbed on the horses and took off towards Nevis's palace. Lavasco and Tripper took off ahead of them to catch up with Shavoth.

Wait up Lavasco yelled at Shavoth.

I have to get my wife back I will kill him if her harms one hair on her head. And just what are you going to do? Lavasco asked.

I'll think of something. And he is going to get his. Shavoth said.

And you will die in the process. Lavasco said. You don't know what Nevis will do and right now your not thinking straight and that will get you killed. Lavasco said as he caught up to Shavoth. Let's wait for Elphany and the rest of them to catch up. Then we can figure out what to do.

All right Shavoth said. I'm not going to lose my wife. She is the only thing that keeps the light going in my eyes. I couldn't live without her.

I know. Lavasco said and we will not let anything happen to her. I promise you that.

Let's get off these horses and let them rest for a while. Lavasco said.

They climbed off. About ten minutes went by. Shavoth was pacing back and forth. We should have stayed with you and the rest.

It's not your fault we all thought Nevis was on his way back to the palace. Lavasco said.

Elphany came riding up with the rest of the help. We need to get there now. Elphany said.

Wait let's figure out a plan first if we go in there now he will be waiting for us. And going in there with fear will kill all of us. Lavasco said.

We are going to stop Nevis and get my daughter back I am not going to let him destroy anyone or anything else. Elphany said.

But if I go with you he will kill all of us Joe looked at Elphany.

You are not leaving my side you are the one that I love. Elphany said. Succoth came running up to them with the rest of whom he could get. There were a lot of people coming from the road and the woods.

When Elphany looked down the road she could see that there were at least a hundred people if not more to help them.

All right let's go Elphany said. As she grabbed her ankle bracelet, and stretched it out into a sword.

Lavasco looked at Shavoth don't worry if Tarah is as good with her powers as I think she is. She will be able to hold her own.

And I still have my powers. With both of us we can stop Nevis. Elphany said. So since we have enough help let's go. Shavoth said.

Joe grabbed Elphany's hand and kissed it and I shall be there to help. Even if I die I will protect my family.

They all took of towards Nevis's palace with all the help behind them. Jahdson went down to Elphany's lab looked around there were potions for everything. Back on earth people would call her a witch.

There on a shelf he had seen a book when he picked it up. He could see that it was a book on spells. He opened it and it had Elphany's handwriting on it. This could help.

Then he started reading through it. Here we are he found what he was looking for.

He gathered everything together for what he needed. Started adding everything together.

I hope this works he didn't have time to test it out.

He looked around and seen a leather bag. Lying on the table. He put a bunch of potions in it. Put the bag in his bag pack and went up to get some food to take with him.

The maid walked into and saw what he was doing. This is not a good idea that you go with them. She said. Well I am going to go help my parents and sister. Jahdson said.

He walked out of the palace and set out towards Nevis's palace.

CHAPTER 7

Lavasco and Tripper rode up ahead of everyone. They came up on Remus's cabin. Lavasco stopped and got off his horse.

Went into the cabin. Someone is in there walking back out. Climbed back on his horse and said the place is all tore up.

They took off down the road. Looked back and seen a mile down the road here came Elphany and everyone else.

Well I guess we have more then enough help. Tripper said.

We have to get Tarah away from him or no one will ever be safe. Lavasco said. They took off running the horses harder.

They made it to the end of the lane where Nevis's palace was and stopped. We are going to have to walk from here. Lavasco said and climbed off his horse.

Tripper did the same.

Elphany came up from behind. Did you see Tarah yet? She asked. No but I think its best if we walk the rest of the way. Lavasco said.

They started walking till the palace came into view. Wait here I will be right back.

He started walking up to the palace then went behind the tree when he saw the knights out front standing guard.

Then he darted in and out of bushes. Tripper was right behind him. Lavasco pulled out his sword looked behind him I told you to stay back there now go back and tell everyone to start surrounding the palace and stay as far back as they can knowing Nevis he has people posted all over the grounds.

Tripper went back and told everyone what Lavasco had said.

Everyone scattered around the grounds of the palace.

Elphany and Joe followed Tripper back to where Lavasco was. With Shavoth right behind them. Do you see Tarah? He asked.

No not yet. Lavasco said. But T know she is here somewhere. The horses are over there and pointed in the direction of where the horses were.

So he had just got here then. Shavoth said. As far as I can see he did. Lavasco answered.

Well then lets go I am going to go get my daughter. Elphany told everyone.

Wait we have to find a way to get in there. Lavasco said. If we get to impatient it can jeopardize everything. Nevis put Tarah in the lab and tied her to the chair. Soon my dear I will have revenge on your mother and we will be married and I will have all the power over the whole universe.

He brushed her cheek lightly with the back of his hand. Thinking of how beautiful she was. Thinking of how beautiful she was. And no one can stop me now. He went out and told the maid to go get the preacher.

She took off out the door without looking back. And went to go get the preacher.

Then he went up to check on Rosey. She was still asleep so he went in and changed his clothes. Tarah woke up. What am I doing here? Tried to stand up but she sat back down and looked down at her arms and legs.

Who tied me up? Oh no she looked around the room. What happened? I wish these ropes off. At that the ropes disappeared. Now how do I find my way-out of here. I hope Shavoth is alright. She said

Nevis went back down to the lab. When he opened the door he had seen that Tarah was free from the ropes. Standing by the chair.

Go ahead try and leave. You will never see your family again. He said. What did you do to them and where is Shavoth. She asked.

He's dead and if you do as I say no one else will get hurt. Nevis told her. Tarah felt helpless. She sat down in the chair and started crying. Why are you doing this? You killed your own son do you have no shame what so ever? I have done nothing to you she said.

No you haven't done anything. But you have something that I want. And I am going to get it. Nevis said. Now you are free to walk around the palace. But I am going to warn you if you even think about trying to escape the ones that are the closest to you will die. Put that dress on over there he pointed in front of her. Then walked out of the room.

Tarah sat there crying. I have to do something even if my husband is gone. I still have to stop Nevis. Tarah stood up and put the dress on. Looking in the mirror it was a wedding dress I will not marry this man. She noticed that she still had the jewelry on. Well he doesn't know about these then. She said.

I must hide somewhere until I can figure this out. Then she walked out of the lab and up the stairs Walking through the palace and found a room off of the kitchen.

Someone was coming. She didn't have time to hide so she grabbed her breath and made herself disappear. Nevis walked by I know you are here somewhere. Its time for our wedding my dear.

Where are you? Nevis yelled. If you don't come out you will never see you family alive again. Tarah stood there afraid to move as he walked right by her.

You are going to pay for this when I find you no one hides from me and gets away with it. He walked outside raised his right hand in the air, pointed his finger and a bolt of lightening shot through the air. Tarah shivered at the sight of what he had done.

Then walked down the hallway. This is not the end of things it is going to worse for everyone now. Nevis said.

Shavoth started running for the palace when he heard Nevis yelling.

Lavasco ran after him and tackle Shavoth to the ground, don't be a fool. Lavasco said Nevis would rather kill you right now.

Well so much for our plan. Elphany said.

She motioned for everyone to charge the palace. They storm the palace looking for Tarah.

They all took off in different directions. Find my daughter. Elphany yelled. Nevis heard the noise and came running out.

When he had seen all the people come running in. he tried to fire his lightening again dam I need to let it charge. So all he could do is start running for his lab. When he got in there he bolted the door shut.

Within a few seconds Lavasco was right behind him and kicked the door in. he kicked it so hard that it went flying across the room.

Nevis pointed his finger at Lavasco but Lavasco dodged it just in time the bolt of lightening hit the wall. Nevis grabbed a sword right next to him.

Lavasco pulled his out and they started banging swords together. You betrayed me. Nevis yelled at Lavasco.

Yes and I would do it again if I had to. You are an evil man. Lavasco yelled back. And as far as I am concerned you are not my brother anymore.

Nevis was even madder then ever. He pointed hi finger and a bolt of lightening shot out at Lavasco. Hitting him in the arm.

Shavoth came running in.

Look out Lavasco turned at Shavoth.

He jumped out of the way before the bolt of lightening bolt could hit him.

Shavoth ran at Nevis. So you are my son. If that's what you want to call me you can forget it. I don't need someone like you to be my father.

Where is my wife and my mother? Shavoth yelled.

Your mother is somewhere safe and Tarah is going to be my wife. Not yours. Nevis yelled back.

I am taking my wife and mother. No one want to stay with an evil man like you. You are going to pay for the way you treated my other and for kidnapping my wife. Shavoth yelled.

Tarah came running in. Nevis seen her and ran to her.

Shavoth pulled his sword out and stabbed Nevis in the back of the arm

Nevis turned and a ball of fire at Shavoth. Tarah bent down and unhooked her ankle bracelet and made a sword out of it. We need to get out of here the place is going to burn down Lavasco yelled. Tripper came running in. Lavasco told Tripper to go get everyone out of the place was on fire.

Tarah went after Nevis with her sword. Nevis knew he was out numbered do he wrapped his cape around him and disappeared.

Where did he go? Tarah said looking all around the room.

No one saw him anywhere in the room. Lets get this fire out Lavasco said I am going to take this place back I want it in one piece.

When they had the fire out. Shavoth grabbed Tarah and hugged her I am so glad you are ok. Me to Tarah said. Nevis told me you were dead.

I will never let him bluff me again. Tarah said.

They Walked out the door.

Elphany came running in and said Tarah oh my baby she grabbed Tarah and gave her a hug and kiss on the cheek.

All of a sudden they heard a scream. That sounds like Joe. Elphany was running towards where the screams came from. Looked and saw !Joe lying on the floor. oh no Elphany screamed and ran to Joe. She saw blood came running out of Joes arm. Who did this? Elphany asked as she tore a piece of cloth off of her shirt and wrapped it around the wound

It was Nevis Joe said.

Nevis was standing over the top of Elphany. I see you have come back to me. Nevis whispered in Elphany's ear. Elphany jumped and turned around.

No one is going Lo gel. out of here alive. lam going to destroy everyone and this planet. Do you understand? Nevis asked Elphany.

We will see about that. Elphany said

Tarah came running in how can you be so cruel? Tarah yelled when she seen her father on the floor. Nevis grabbed Tarah now you are going to be my bride

Shavoth came running in. Nevis pointed his finger at Shavoth. Shavoth stood there froze he couldn't move.

Tarah reached up and adjusted her necklace all of a sudden Nevis let go. You are going to pay for that. Succoth came running in and jumped Nevis from behind.

Nevis was struggling with the beast, Nevis got one of his hands free reached in his pocket and grabbed some sleeping powder and blew it at Succoth. Succoth fell on the floor fast asleep.

Tripper came in after Lavasco. Get Joe out of here Lavasco told Tripper.

Tripper ran over and helped Joe to his feet and they took off out of the palace.

Nevis looked at everyone grabbed Tarah and wrapped is cape around both of them and disappeared in a fog of smoke

Where are they? Elphany asked. They started running thought the palace looking through every room no one was around anywhere. Shavoth went up to Nevis's room looked on the bed and there was his mother sound asleep.

He went over and woke her up. She looked at him. Shavoth what are you doing here? You must hide before Nevis sees you.

It is to late he has already seen me. And now he has Tarah we must find her Shavoth said. No he can't he is supposed to be with me Rosey stood up out of bed and was to weak.

She sat back to lay down I am sorry Shavoth I cannot go anywhere right now. No he can't he is supposed to be with me. Rosey got up out of bet but was to weak to go anywhere.

Did he do this to you? Shavoth asked.

No he has been taking care of me. It was one of the knights that did this to me and Nevis took care of him.

I can carry you out of here. Shavoth said. No you go find Tarah I will be ok. Rosey told Shavoth. All right mother. But I don't like leaving you alone here. Shavoth said.

Rosey lay there crying he lied to me he doesn't care about me at all.

Nevis had Tarah locked in a room in the tower and put a spell on the room so no one could get in or out but him. He walked out locking the door behind him.

Let me out you fool. Tarah screaming.

Tarah looked around there was a window that looked out onto the bay no way to climb out at all now what do I do? Tarah asked. Nevis left her up there by herself. Tarah was pounding on the door saying let me out over and over. But no one was there. Elphany, Lavasco and Shavoth met outside. Tarah was no where to be found.

Where is she Elphany said?

No one could find her at all.

Well let's let everyone go home. Elphany said there is nothing else to do for now.

He won't kill her right now. They walked out and told everyone thanks for helping and they could Leave. They all started walking along the path and disappeared in the woods. Now what do we do? Shavoth asked.

I have no idea where he has taken Tarah. Nevis snuckNevis snuck in through the kitchen and went up the back stairs to his room. Rosey heard him coming and pretended that she was still asleep. Nevis walked in looked at Rosey. Good she is still sleeping.

Went in the bathroom and cleaned his wounds.

When he was done he left the room thinking Rosey was still asleep. Went into the library and sat down and wrote a letter.

It said Elphany if you want to see Tarah alive you will do as I say meet me were we first met then you will get your daughter back and if you don't I will destroy your daughter and everyone else along with her.

Nevis sat there thinking if I can get both Elphany and Tarah together that will be twice the power that I need.

He put the not in an envelope and walked out to see where they had went. Looked out the window and seen them walking towards the forest.

He called for the knight take this to Elphany and hurry. And come back to let me know if she received it.

The knight bowed and took off out the door after Elphany when he caught up to her he handed her the note Shavoth and Lavasco drew their swords at the knight.

Elphany grabbed the letter and said wait let him go. You two go on I will join you later. Elphany said. No we are not letting you go alone· Both Shavoth and Lavasco said at the same time. I insist you do otherwise Tarah will die. Now go home. And let Joe know what is going on and tell him that I love him

But Elphany you can't go alone he will kill you.

No he won't deep down inside he still loves me. I will be ok. Elphany said. Go this time I demand you to go home. Elphany said.

Elphany turned around and went back to talk to Nevis.

Why couldn't he let things go she said to herself now he is out to destroy everything in his path? I have to find a way to stop him. Elphany was saying to herself.

Shavoth looked at Lavasco we can't let her go alone can we?

No but let's wait till she gets there then we will follow her. Lavasco answered. The knight went back and told Nevis Elphany is on her way to see you.

Nevis walked out to the garden and sat down where he and Elphany first met. Remembering the first time he fell in love with Elphany thinking of how beautiful she was.

That is never going to happen between us again but now I will have my revenge and I will enjoy doing it. Nevis said to himself.

Elphany walked up ok Nevis I am here now let my daughter go free.

That's not why I asked you here. You and Tarah are going to help me. So let's go. He stood up and started walking towards the tower.

As they got closer to the tower. Elphany spoke up why my daughter why not me just let her go.

Never I need the both of you. Nevis said.

You know I have the power to stop you right now? Elphany asked.

He turned around and looked at her and before you do that your daughter will be dead. Nevis said.

Let her go now Elphany screamed.

Nevis stopped grabbed her by the hair and stuck his face into hers. Don't you ever raise your voice to me ever? Then he slapped her.

Elphany put her hand on here face. Nevis just stood there and looked at her. At that he looked at her like he was sorry he had done that.

Then he kissed her on the lips. Just like the first time he had kissed her before.

Passion flew up inside of him. Elphany tried to get away but he was too strong. Nevis reached in his cape and grabbed some green powder and sprinkled it on her. The powder only last about a half an hour. But that was long enough for him.

All at once she forgot that it wasn't the past she started kissing him back.

Oh Nevis don't go to war I will never see you again.

They fell to the ground and made love. When they were done Nevis said. Now that I have you I will never let you go.

Elphany looked at him. She was starting to come back. Nevis knew it and stood up lets go time is running out.

They walked the steps in the tower up to the room where Tarah was. Nevis reversed the spell so they could go in.

Tarah was in there sitting on the window ledge. Seen her mother walk in and went running over to her. Oh mommy why is all this happening? How are we going to get out of this?

Don't worry I will think of something to get us out of here. Elphany said. You really think that you will be able to get away now? Nevis said.

Yes I do Elphany said.

Well we will see about that and Nevis closed the door and locked it then he said the spell that no one could change.

Shavoth and Lavasco crept back in to the palace. Looked allover the place. Elphany was nowhere inside. So they went outside and walked the grounds.

Shavoth grabbed Lavasco's arm look. They went and hid behind a hedge and watched Nevis come out of the garden.

When he gets out of site lets go in there. Elphany and Tarah must be out by the garden somewhere.

What *is* out there besides the garden? Shavoth asked.

There's a couple of sheds and the at the same time both Shavoth and Lavasco said the tower.

That's where Nevis put them. Nevis disappeared inside house and Shavoth and. Lavasco took off. towards the tower. There was a Knight out there standing guard to stop us. Shavoth said.

They took off towards the tower and came up behind him tapped him on the shoulder and when they did both Lavasco and Shavoth hit him and knocked him out. Lavasco drug him around the side of the tower tied him up and put a gag in his mouth.

Then they went in the tower they climbed the stairs when they got to the door.

They yelled Tarah, Elphany are you in there? we are but Nevis put a spell on the tower so we can't get out. What are we going to do? Shavoth asked.

Lets both make a wish at the same time Elphany said. They said we wish to be out of the tower at the same time.

At that they were standing on the other side of the door.

I am so glad to see you. Tarah said to Shavoth. Let's get out of here. Elphany said.

Wait a minute don't you think we should put some look-alikes in there so we can get out of here. Tarah said.

Your right Elphany said. I wish to have a clone of me in the tower. Elphany said.

Tarah wished for the same thing. And these ones can't talk.

All right lets go. Elphany said.

They went down the stairs and took off towards the wood the back way.

Nevis was making his way back to the tower.

Where is the guard? He asked. he went around the tower there was the knight bound and gagged.

Nevis asked the guard what happened. Nevis was so mad he didn't even finish untying the guard. He ran up the stairs and went inside good their sleeping they didn't get out. Nevis said.

Then he went out locked the door. Went down the stairs and outside. Put a spell on the tower.

Then walked to the palace. I need to get some sleep. He said to himself. So he went upstairs to his room. Went in and took a bath. Then went and climbed in bed.

Rosey rolled over. Where have you been? She asked. Out walking the grounds that's all. Nevis answered. Rosey wrapped her arms around Nevis, I love you she said.

I love you to. And gave her a kiss on the cheek. Then he fell fast asleep.

Elphany, Tarah, Shavoth and Lavasco were walking back to their home.

How long do you think it will take before Nevis realizes that its not us in the tower? Tarah asked. That I cant say but he does he is going to be angry.

Elphany was really quit walking home. She was thinking of Nevis. Why do I have these feelings for him? I am in love with my husband not Nevis but I have some kind of feelings towards him and I can't figure it out. She brushed it off for a while. I was thinking the next time we run into Nevis we need to be together. Tarah said.

Your right Elphany said. It is stronger if we stay together. They made it to the horses climbed on them and took off towards home. Halfway along the path they ran into Jahdson.

What are you doing here? Elphany asked. Looking for you. Jahdson answered.

You were supposed to stay at home. Elphany said. Yes I know but I found something that we could use. He replied.

Well lets go home and see what you have done. She said. Yes mom but what I found we have to go see Nevis. Jahdson said

Not now son I am tired and I want to go home so lets go. Jahdson climbed on the horse behind Elphany and they rode home.

Jahdson tried to talk to his mother but she kept quite all the way home. After they returned home. Elphany said I am going up to check on Joe. Then told the butler to put the invisible wall up. And then went to her room.

The butler bowed and did as she said.

What is wrong with mom? Jahdson asked Tarah.

I don't know. She has been acting like this since Nevis locked her in the tower with me. Tarah answered. Well we are going to have to :figure out what is going on with her. Lavasco said.

I wonder if Nevis put a spell on Elphany. Shavoth said.

That I am not sure of but she sure is acting different. Lavasco said.

Elphany checked on Joe laying in the bed. Went over and kissed him on the cheek. Tarah is back with us my love. How is your arm? She asked.

It's alright just a little sore. Joe answered. that's good I'm going to go take a bath, kissed Joe on the cheek and went into the bathroom. Joe notice something different about Elphany she wasn't acting herself at all.

In the morning I will ask Tarah and Shavoth what has happened. Joe said.

Elphany was sitting in the tub. What is this feeling that I have for Nevis.?

I love Joe dearly and he is my life but I want to be with. Nevis. Why do I feel this way now?

She got out of the bath,. grabbed her robe and put in on and went back into the bedroom. Sat down at the vanity and took her hair out of the bun. Here hair flowed all the way down past her ankles it was golden blonde. When she looked in the mirror she looked just like Tarah.

Joe climbed out of bed went over to her grabbed the brush and started brushing her hair looking at her in the mirror. She had a sad look on her face.

You know I love you with all my heart Epiphany. Is there something wrong? He asked.

Things will be all right by morning looking at him through the. Mirror she could see the concern in his eyes. She took the brush from Joe laid it down on the vanity and stood up.

Joe gently grabbed her by the hand and walked her to the bed. They climbed in bed and Joe leaned over and kissed her on the lips he noticed right away that she was acting different when she didn't kiss him back the way she usually did. He raised his head up and looked in her eyes are you sure there is nothing wrong my dear? Joe asked.

No I am just tired that's all. Ok well goodnight lets get some sleep. Joe said. That sounds great to me. Elphany said.

Joe rolled over and said to himself she is not herself. I am going to get to the bottom of this. Then he fell asleep. Elphany laid there for a long time thinking of Joe and Nevis not knowing what to do.

What is wrong with me? Elphany asked. Then fell of to asleep.

Tarah and Shavoth went upstairs to their room climbed into bed Shavoth wrapped his arms around Tarah and said I love you so much kissed her on the lips and she told him the same. And both fell asleep. Meanwhile Lavasco and Jahdson sat downstairs in the kitchen eating a snack.

I have something her that will stop Nevis. But I need to get to his lab so I can. Jahdson said. And if you do that Nevis will kill you. Lavasco said so you are not going and that's an order. You just leave this up to the grownups.

Yes but I can do it. Jahdson said. And you can get hurt really bad you are not going and that's it. Lavasco said. Ok well I am going up to bed I am tired. Jahdson stood up and started walking up to his room. Lets wait until everyone get up in the morning then we can talked to everyone about it. Lavasco said.

Alright I am going up to bed then. Jahdson said. And headed off up to his room.

Nevis woke up thinking of what he was going to do next. Looked over and seen that Rosey wasn't in the bed. He jumped up out of bed to see where she was. Looked in the bathroom and she wasn't there. Then he ran downstairs. She was sitting in the kitchen drinking.

You scared me I thought you left. Nevis said. No I am still here. She said. I just had an upset stomach so I went to get something for it. I am fine now.

Nevis sat down in the chair next to her and kissed her on the cheek. I am going for a walk would you like to go with me? He asked.

No I think I will sit here for a while. Rosey said.

Nevis stood up kissed on the cheek again and walked out onto the patio. Rosey watched as he walked out and down the path. I am going to leave when I get better. I have had enough. Even though I love him with all my heart I cannot stay and watch him destroy everything I just wish I could stop him somehow.

Nevis walked towards the tower. Now I know Elphany will be mine and with the spell I put on her. She is falling in love with me again.

Nevis walked up the stairs of the tower. Took the spell off the tower and walked in lit a candle that was on the table and walked over to Elphany and Tarah now that I have you locked in here for a while are you going to do as I say.

They just sat there and starred at him. Listen to me I will leave you up here to starve if you don't do as I say. Nevis was getting madder by the minute, walked over and grabbed Elphany by the hair and pulled her up to him with her toes dangling on the floor. Looked at her into her eyes you will do as I say. She just bad a blank look on her face.

Your not Elphany and threw her across the room. He went over and picked up Tarah looked her in the eyes and your not Tarah. And threw her on top of Elphany.

They tricked me. Nevis raised his fists in the air pointed his finger and lightening went through the room putting a bole in the wall. I will have what I want and I will not stop this time till I get what I want. From this day on everyone and everything will be destroyed until I get what I want. He pointed his finger at the two woman on the floor a bolt of lightening shot out and both of them turned to dust.

He stormed out of the tower they will be back I shall make sure of that. Nevis yelled.

He walked back to the palace. Went down to his lab and started working on a new potion.

Elphany woke the next morning feeling not feeling at all her normal self. She shook Joe to wake him up. Joe looked up at her still sleepy. Are you alright? He asked.

No I am not I feel awful I think I will stay in bed today I fell awful I think I will stay in bed today. Elphany said.

I'll go down and see if breakfast is ready and go get us some at that he got up out of bed put his clothes on and went down to see if anyone was up.

Lavasco was sitting in the chair flirting with the maid.

Good morning everyone. Joe said walking into the kitchen. Well good morning Lavasco and said. Joe ordered the maid to fix him and Elphany some breakfast.

Have you noticed anything different about Elphany? Lavasco asked.

I don't know but she isn't acting like herself at all. Do you know what happened after I left? Joe asked. Lavasco told Joe everything that had happened.

Well I think that Nevis put a spell on her. Joe said. that's what I was thinking. She was acting really strange all the way home. Lavasco said.

You know dad if Nevis put a spell on mom I can reverse it. Jahdson said. Walking into the room. There is a room downstairs with potions and everything in it. Joe said. But you be careful on what you are doing with that stuff down there. Joe said.

I am going with him and make sure he doesn't blow himself up. Lavasco said.

The made finished putting the food on the tray and started walking up the stairs to the master bedroom.

Joe was right behind her.

Joe opened the door for her and told her where to put the tray.

Then he went over and opened the curtains and said okay breakfast is here. Elphany are you awake? He asked and turned around.

Elphany isn't in the bed master. The maid said.

Go down and see if she might be in the kitchen. And i will look for her up here.

If you cant find her get everyone together I think I know where she went. Joe said.

The maid ran out of the room and ran downstairs. Looking in the kitchen and the rest of the bouse. Joe grabbed a few bites of his food.

He went and looked in the bathroom and she was nowhere to be found. Then walked in the closet and she wasn't there but seen that she had changed into her best dress.

Where are you Elphany? Joe asked. She needs to be in bed she is sick

Joe went downstairs and went down to the lab. Did Elphany come this way? Joe asked Lavasco and Jahdson.

No we have been busy down here since we left the kitchen. Lavasco told Joe.

I am almost done with this potion. I just need to do a few more things. Jahdson said. Lets go and see if we can find Elphany. Lavasco said.

Lavasco and Joe took off up the stairs and out to the stable and seen there was a horse missing. Maybe Tarah and Shavoth went for a ride. Lavasco said.

No they would have took two horses Joe said.

The went out to the garden and asked the gardener if he had seen Elphany.

No I haven't yet this morning. But if I do I will tell her you are looking for her. The gardener answered. Okay thanks Joe said.

You didn't see the way she was acting this morning. Joe told Lavasco. It was like she was in a different place and time. Joe had a worried look on his face. What if she doesn't want to be found? Joe asked.

Ok my friend we will go look for her. And for her not to want to be with her family that doesn't sound like her. You are her whole world Joe so you need to get that out of your head right now. Lets go get Tarah and Shavoth. And see what they say. Lavasco said.

Tarah and Shavoth were out on the patio having breakfast. Cuddling close to each other on the lounge chair. When Joe and Lavasco came out to them. Joe went up to Tarah and told her what was going on. Without a second thought Tara jumped out of the lounge chair almost dumping Shavoth on the ground, let's go get mommy. She said. They all went out to the stable and saddled the horses and started to take off. When Jahdson came running out I have it now lets go get mom. And I have a big surprise for Nevis in this bag. Holing it up in the air.

Ok Lavasco said climb on. They all started riding towards the palace when they seen that the invisible wall was down. Elphany must of forgot to put it back up. So Lavasco got off the horse and went over to a panel and turned a knob and the wall came sliding up. Then rode up to the rest of them

Nevis was in the lab looking through the crystal ball. Saying come to me now Elphany. I can se you coming to me. And soon you will bring Tarah with you for I know she is out looking for you. Then he laughed an evil laugh. I will have what I want and soon I will be able to rule the universe. Watching Elphany in the crystal ball. He was laughing so loud it echoed throughout the palace. And everyone held their hands over their ears and started crying. They knew that they were helpless with the powers he had.

Elphany was riding down the rode thinking of Nevis. Why am I having these feelings towards him its like I just want to be with him now more then ever. What did he do to me? I know I love Joe more then life itself. But there is something attracting me to him. And I cant shake it off.

Tarah led the way pushing her horse hard to run faster. The others were right behind her. It didn't take long for them to catch up to Elphany. Joe was yelling Elphany wait. Elphany turned around and seen everyone running their horses to catch up to her.

Nevis was really mad now. that's it they have stopped me for the last time I am going out there to them. He screamed. I am going to bring the both of them back with me and if have to kill them I will but not till after I drain an of their powers. He tore out of the lab knocking everything over in the process by the time he got outside the palace was in shambles. Ordered the knight to saddle up his horse. When the knight brought the horse out Nevis ordered him to get more men and meet him at Elphany's. got on his horse and took off.

Joe was arguing with Elphany to come back home with him but all she would say is I am sorry Joe I have to do this I have no choice. Tarah rode up please I want you to come home with us. don't let Nevis win. But I have to go Elphany said. I think Nevis put a spell on you Elphany. Lavasco said.

Well I can change that Tarah said. And wished for the spell to be reversed. Elphany started swaying on her horse and almost fell off when Joe caught her. She looked up at Joe and all around. Where am I? she asked. Thank you Tarah. Now lets go home. Joe said.

Nevis was on his way to Elphany's I am not leaving until I get what I want this time. The knights were right behind him. I want everyone killed but Elphany and Tarah and if you don't do it I will kin each of you. Do you understand. They all shook their heads. Now go. Nevis yelled.

I have to put another spell on both Elphany and Tarah. And this time they are going to give me what I want.

Why was I going towards Nevis's? Elphany asked.

He put a spell to get you to go to him. Tarah answered. Well that's why I was acting really strange. Elphany said. lets just go home we need to get prepared. Nevis is going to try again. This time they were unaware of what was just about to happen. The knight came up from behind and hit Lavasco in the back of the head with the butt of the sword.

Lavasco fell off the horse unconscious. Shavoth jumped off his horse and drew his sword.

Joe did the same. Elphany and Tarah reached down and grabbed their ankle bracelets and stretched them out into swords.

When is this going to stop? Elphany asked.

When Nevis gets what he wants the knight said. They started clashing swords. Joe was laying on the ground unconscious. And Shavoth was stabbed in the stomach.

While Elphany and Tarah was fighting two of the knights.

Two others came up from behind and wrapped them up in ropes.

Elphany and Tarah dropped their swords. The knights put them on the horses and took off towards Nevis's. now I guess you two are going to do as Nevis says. And they took off. Halfway down the road they ran into Nevis. This is it was easier then I thought it would be. Nevis said.

Let's go it won't be long now and I will have what I want. Nevis said.

I am going to stop you once and for all. Elphany screamed.

And just how do you think your going to do that? You two are tied up. Nevis said.

Just you wait and see. I will have you dead before noon tomorrow. Elphany said. Nevis didn't say a word he just reached out and slapped her right across the mouth. Blood started seeping out of Elphany's lips. She didn't say a word the rest of the way. Tarah looked at Nevis trying to untie her ropes. Nevis saw what she was doing took out a knife and pointed at her throat. Take off the ropes and you will die. When they got to the palace Nevis told the knight to take them to the tower and chain them up in different rooms I will be out later I have a few things to do first. Then walked into the palace.

Lavasco was just waking up. Rubbing his head he looked around. Oh no they can't be dead. He went over to Joe he had a knot on his head but he was still alive. Lavasco shook him and woke him up. Oh that hurts rubbing his head. Joe said. Lavasco Went over to Shavoth. He was still alive but had a deep wound in his stomach and was losing a lot of blood.

We must get him home and get this wound taking care of. Lavasco took his shirt off and wrapped 't around Shavoth to stop the bleeding. Then he helped him on his horse. Went over and helped Joe on his horse. And climbed on his and they took off towards home.

When they got there the butler came running out get him in and take care of his wounds. Lavasco said. He climbed off his horse. And helped Shavoth off his horse. The butler helped Shavoth inside and helped him in bed and went and got some medicine and needle and thread for His wounds.

When the butler came back Shavoth had passed out. The butler started working on the wounds he was just starting to stitch up the wounds when Shavoth woke up. Here take some of this. What is it? Shavoth moaned.

It's pain medicine it will help you heal faster. The butler said. Shavoth drank it. When he finished he asked where Tarah and Elphany was.

They didn't come back. The butler answered. What I have to go get them, he started to get up and moaned in pain. Shavoth said.

You cant go anywhere in your condition. The butler said. But I must go help them. Shavoth said and fell fast asleep.

The butler finished stitching up Shavoth then went out to help Lavasco with Joe.

The butler gave Joe some pain medicine. Went to hand some to Lavasco but Lavasco refused. Where is Jahdson? Lavasco asked.

He is still in the lab the butler answered.

Lavasco took off to get Jahdson. Jahdson was just finishing the last of what he was making and putting them into the vials.

Are you finished? Lavasco asked.

Yes all done and boy is Nevis going to be surprised when he gets this. Jahdson said. Ok then lets go we have no time to waste. Lavasco said.

Well what are we waiting for? Putting the vials in his back pack lets go. Jahdson said. As he started walking out the door.

Lavasco was right behind him.

They climbed on the horses and took off towards Nevis's palace. When they were almost there Lavasco stopped and motioned for Jahdson to stop.

He climbed off his horse. And said we must walk from here. And I want you to follow close behind me. And don't stray anywhere without me. Lavasco said.

I will lets go. Jahdson said. They crept up to the hedges then sneaking in and out from behind the trees. Lavasco snuck up on a knight and knocked him out. Tied the knight up and gagged him and did the rest to the rest of them.

Ok now its safe to go in. as they crept in Lavasco was watching to make sure no one could see them. They went down to the lab.

Lavasco stood by the door while Jahdson poured the vials into all the potions. Now Nevis wont be able to do anything with these. Jahdson said.

He put the vials back in his pack and looked around the room and seen the crystal ball he put it in his backpack.

What are you doing with that? Lavasco asked. It will come in handy. Jahdson said.

All right lets get out of here before Nevis comes in. Lavasco said.

Lavasco walked out looked around no one was there. They snuck outside. We need to hide somewhere as he looked around he could hear Nevis talking to Rosey out on the terrace. Lets go before he sees us. Lavasco said.

They took off towards a little shed out by the stables. They went inside.

You stay in here and don't come out for any reason until I come back for you. Lavasco said.

Ok J will but wait lets see where mo and Tarah is. He reached in the backpack and grabbed the crystal ball looked inside and asked it where they where. The crystal ball went cloudy then started clearing up it shows two rooms and both of them are chained to the wall. Elphany had blood on her lip. Moms hurt. Jahdson said. Lavasco looked and seen J know where they are hide somewhere I am going to go get them I know where they are. Jahdson did. And Lavasco took off after Elphany and Tarah.

Nevis was holding Rosey's hand I do love you Rosey. And I love you Rosey replied I must tell you something Rosey said

What is it? Nevis asked.

I am three months along with your child. Rosey said. You are Nevis asked. Well this time I will be here for you and he grabbed Rosey and hugged her. That is all I wanted to here. Rosey said.

Lavasco made it to the tower and no one had seen him. I guess all the knights are tied up for the moment. Lavasco said.

He went into the room at the top of the stairs. And broke the door down. Elphany was chained to the wall with a gag in her mouth. There was dried blood on her lips.

Lavasco unchained her and took the gag off. Then they went to get Tarah when they got in the room Tarah was trying to get loose but the chains wouldn't budge.

Lavasco let her loose of the chains. And Tarah took the gag out of her mouth. That man is going to pay. No one hits my mother and gets away with it.

They all walked down the stairs and out into the sunlight.

Let's go home Elphany said.

And they took off running. Lavasco went in the shed and got Jahdson. They all took off running towards the horses.

We going to have to ride double there is only two horses. Lavasco said. He climbed on and helped Elphany on. And Jahdson did the same.

And took off running the horses. When they got horse Lavasco told Elphany and Tarah about what had happened.

Elphany and Tarah took off into the palace to see Joe and Shavoth. Jahdson and Lavasco put the horses away.

Wait till Nevis goes down and tries his potions out. All he will get is it corning back on him.

Let's look in the crystal ball and see what's going on. Lavasco said. They put the horses away and Jahdson took out the crystal ball.

Lavasco looked in the crystal ball. There was Nevis standing talking to Rosey.

Lavasco couldn't believe it. I do think that Nevis does love Rosey. Nevis gave Rosey a hug and walked out to the garden.

There he goes to towards the tower. Jahdson said.

Well let's watch and see what he does. Lavasco said.

As Nevis got closer Lavasco was getting nervous. He will start destroying things this time and kill anyone that he sees. He has to be stopped.

Nevis walked up the stairs to where Elphany was. The door was opened.

Nevis stood there in the room clenching his fists. They are going to pay dearly now. Nevis raised his hand and pointed his finger at everything he had seen. Destroying the whole room.

Then he went in the room where Tarah was. She was gone to. Well this is not going to stop me I will get what I want if I have to destroy everything and everyone that Elphany loves.

He walked back to the palace and went down to his lab. In there he went in to a room off the lab and found the mechanical men that he made when he was younger. He opened the back and adjusted a few wires. And turned on one of them.

He did the same to the rest of them. Follow me he ordered them.

Jahdson and Lavasco looked at each other. We have a huge problem if they get into the palace. Jahdson said.

Yes we do so let's see if the invisible wall is up and all the holes are closed up. Lavasco said.

They ran out of the stable and caught the butler outside talking to one of the maid was hanging clothes.

And Jahdson went and talked to the butler the butler ran in the palace to seeif the invisible wall was up then he went out and ordered the stable hands to fill up all the holes with dirt so nothing could get through. Elphany was laying next to Joe talking to him. When Jahdson" knocked on the door. Elphany said come in. When Jahdson did he told her what was going on.

Well let's get ready for Nevis. Elphany said.

Elphany went and told Tarah what was going on.

Tarah looked at Elphany. I can't leave Shavoth like this he needs me. He needs you to stop Nevis or everyone is going to die. Elphany said. Tarah gave Shavoth a kiss on the cheek and said I will be back as soon as I can.

And I love you. Go save the people of this planet I will be fine now go and save the I am feeling a little better. At that Tarah followed Elphany down to the patio were everyone was sitting.

Joe was arguing with Jahdson. You are not going with us it is too dangerous for you. But dad we need everyone we can get and I have Succoth here to protect me if anything happens. I am going. Jahdson said Elphany stepped in what is it that you can do son. Jahdson showed her his moves with the sword. Who taught you that? Elphany asked. Jahdson didn't say anything. He was afraid to get Lavasco in trouble. I taught him a few things the others he learned on his own. Lavasco said. Elphany looked at Joe. Well I guess our son can hold his own. Joe was a little hesitant but then he gave in we do need everyone we can get. They all started a strategy of what everyone was going to do.

Chapter 8

A few months went by and everything was back to normal. Jahdson was looking through the crystal ball at Nevis. Nevis was down in the lab when the skinny maid came knocking. It is time master. The maid said. Nevis followed the maid up to his room. There was Rosey sitting on the chair you were ready to have the baby. Nevis said.

No it was a false alarm. I just wanted to talk to you. She got up and walked over to the bed to lie down.

Nevis sat on the bed next to her and put his arms around her.

Now that we are together are things going to be better for everyone? Rosey asked. Nevis let go of Rosey and started clenching his fists I am going to make Elphany pay for what she did to me.

But you seem to be happy now that I am here with you and going to have your child.

I am happy being with you Nevis said. But I have to finish what I have started.

Can't you forgive and let them be happy? Rosey asked. She started crying

No I am going to get what I want and you will be there for me. Nevis said.

I hope you don't get upset for what I am going to say. But let go and be the loving person you once were. All these years you have grieved and plotted against Elphany.

It is time to let go. All I have ever wanted was for you to love me the way I love you. Rosey put her hands over her face and started crying.

Nevis started to get angry. I will not stop until I get what I want.

Rosey climbed out of bed and started walking out of the room. Nevis tried to grab her arm but she moved it out of the way.

I didn't say you could leave. Nevis said

I do not care what you say. I am not staying in this room until you decide that it is either me or Elphany that you here one more minute listening to you rant and rave about either her or me. Rosey yelled back.

How dare you talk to me like that? Nevis was screaming now.

I will talk to you the way I want. I am a person not an animal. Rosey snapped back at him.

Jahdson went and got everyone to see and hear what was going on.

As they all came in and watched what was going on with Rosey and Nevis. Elphany sat there well I guess it is about time she told him like it was. And she is with child too. Lavasco said.

That's why she is getting away with talking to him like that. Tarah said. Nevis pointed his finger at Rosey as she walked out of the room.

Nothing happened when Nevis pointed his finger. What's going on? Nevis yelled. I have no powers left.

Well I guess that spell I put on him worked. Jahdson said. Good going everyone said.

You would kill your child Rosey screamed at Nevis.

He pointed his finger at the wall and again nothing happened. Someone *is* going to pay for this. Nevis screamed.

Well now you can't hold anything on me to stay anymore. Rosey said. Please don't leave me. Nevis yelled at Rosey.

I will not leave but I am not staying in the same room with you until you decide what you want. Rosey said.

Nevis sat there thinking for a while I need to do something before she takes my child away from me.

Rosey walked out on him and went down to her room she was tired from arguing with Nevis.

Well that took care of that. Jahdson said. What did you do? Elphany asked.

I changed all his potions and put a spell on him. Jahdson answered her. Well that will only last for a while. Tarah said.

So let us all get prepared. It will happen soon so let's figure out what we all are going to do. Lavasco said.

Nevis sat there thinking for a while he didn't want to lose Rosey and the baby but he was going to get what he wanted in the process.

He got up and walked down to Rosey's room.

As he walked in he saw that she was sleeping. He climbed in bed with her and held her. I am sorry I don't want to lose you or the baby I promise things will be better. Nevis said.

Rosey turned over. That's all I wanted to hear and kissed him on the lips.

They laid there holding each other for a while. I love you so much. Rosey said. And I you. Nevis answered her.

Well Nevis is up to something. It will be a while before he does anything now. Elphany said.

Let's leave them alone now. Tarah said.

Jahdson put the crystal ball up. Tarah went up to her room to check on. Shavoth. He was laying there awake. Tarah could see that he was worried.

You don't have anything to worry about right now. Tarah sat down in a chair at the edge of the bed. Told Shavoth what had happened?

So my mother is going to have another her child. Shavoth said.

Nevis climbed out of bed I have to make her think that I am not going to do anything. He went up to his parents room. Looked around on one wall was a large painting of his parents they were looking each other smiling. They looked so much in love. or anywhere around you want. I cannot stay here anymore it's the baby.

Stay here for a while. Please give me one more chance. And she kissed him on the lips. I love you so much. Rosey said.

On another wall was a painting of Nevis, Lavasco and his parents. That was some happy times. Nevis said.

He looked around the room and seen his mothers jewelry box. Opened the box. There was beautiful music coming out of it.

There were necklaces and bracelets and rings in the box. He picked up one of the rings and took it down to Rosey.

When he walked in Rosey was sitting in bed she had tears in her eyes. What is wrong? Nevis asked.

I thought you lied to me. Rosey answered.

Nevis walked over to the bed got down on her knees and grabbed he left hand. Rosey will you have the pleasure of being my wife? Nevis asked. As he put the ring on her finger.

Rosey looked at the ring it had a huge diamond on it. This is your mothers ring

I cannot accept this. Rosey said.

Yes you can. Mother would have wanted you to have it. Nevis said.

Then yes I will be happy to be your wife. Rosey said. She gave Nevis a long kiss on the lips.

A sharp pain rose up in her stomach. She let go of Nevis and grabbed her stomach.

What's wrong? Nevis said.

I think it's time. Rosey said. What do you mean? Nevis asked.

I think the baby is coming. Rosey said. What do I do? Nevis asked.

Get the maid to go after the doctor. Something is not right. Rosey said. Nevis ran out and yelled to the maid to get the doctor.

The maid ran out after the doctor.

It hurts real badly. Its not the same as the first something is wrong it doesn't feel right. Rosey said.

Nevis paced the floor for a while. He went over and took her in his arms please don't let anything happen to Rosey and the baby. Nevis said.

Rosey looked at Nevis. I will not leave you and the baby will be alright. I promise. Rosey said.

The doctor came in. I must ask you to leave so I can examine Rosey. Nevis was hesitant but for Rosey and the child he left the room.

Nevis stayed outside the room pacing the floor. About three hours went by all of a sudden there was a cry coming from the room.

The doctor yelled out. Nevis you can come in now. Nevis came running in the room.

You have a beautiful little girl. And her mother is fine. The doctor said. Thank you for helping her out. The maid came in with a washbasin and washed the baby and the mother up.

Nevis told the maid to fix the doctor something to eat and bring something for him and Rosey.

He gave the doctor some jewels and sent him on his way.

Nevis went over to Rosey. She was holding the baby in her arms. Her is your daughter as Rosey handed the baby to Nevis.

Nevis looked at the baby with such love in his eyes.

I will be there for you always I promise I will make it up to you for all the harm I have put on you. And if my son will forgive me for not wanting him around I will have the family that I have always wanted.

Nevis handed the baby back to Rosey. And kissed Rosey on the cheek. The maid came in with the tray of food.

Nevis told the maid to bring a bed for the baby in his room. Rosey put the baby on the bed and put a cover on top of the baby. Then her and Nevis ate their lunch.

They ate in silence both of them afraid to say anything to the other they were too happy.

When they were finished eating. Nevis picked up the baby. You stay right there I will be right back. Nevis told Rosey. He took the baby in his room and laid her in the crib.

Then he went back and picked Rosey up and carried her to his room. This is were you belong. Nevis said.

Please don't leave me again I promise I will try and change. I will never leave you for anything. Rosey said.

Nevis laid Rosey on the bed.

The baby started crying. Nevis went and picked the baby up and she was still crying.

What's wrong with the child? Nevis asked.

She is probably hungry. Rosey answered. As she held her arms out for the baby. Nevis handed the baby to Rosey and she put the baby to her breast and fed her. What are we going to name her? Nevis asked.

How about Katy Rose? Rosey asked.

Yes that sounds good that is a beautiful name. Nevis answered.

Well my mother will be all right now I am so glad that Nevis lost his powers even if it is for a short time. Can you ask Jahdson to bring the crystal ball in so I can see my mother? Shavoth asked.

Tarah went out and got Jahdson.

When they came back in Shavoth was up walking around. I feel so much better. That medicine you gave me has worked. Shavoth said.

That's great Tarah said and gave him a kiss on the cheek.

Jahdson sat the crystal ball down on the table and they all sat around and looked through the crystal ball.

We must have a wedding at the end of the week you should be feeling better by then. Nevis was holding Rosey.

You really mean it? Rosey asked.

Yes there is nothing I want more then to have you as my wife.

I just hope that your son can be here to see the wedding. Nevis said. And see the change in you. Rosey said.

I promise you things will be better I will make you a good home with me. Nevis said.

And you are going to forgive Elphany for everything? Rosey asked.

Yes as long as I have you to love I will give up my quest for revenge. Nevis said.

Shavoth looked at Tarah and then at Jahdson. I hope he will fulfill his promise. Cause if he doesn't I will kill him myself. Shavoth said.

What a beautiful sister you have. Tarah said.

Yes she is isn't she? Shavoth said.

I will send out invitations. Rosey said.

Send one to our son if he will forgive me for the way I treated you and him.

I cannot change what I did in the past but I will prove that I will make up for all the hurt I have caused.

I love you so much. Rosey said.

And I love you with all my heart. Nevis said.

Shavoth looked at Tarah do you think he has changed? Shavoth asked. It sure looks like it to me. Tarah answered.

He seems to be happy. We will see if he is going to change. Shavoth said. We are invited to the wedding and he has lost his powers. Shavoth said. Are you sure we should go? Tarah asked.

He does look like he's happy. Jahdson said.

Well I guess only time will tell. But we will have to keep our eyes open to what is going on. Shavoth said.

Yes we will. Tarah said.

Let's go outside I have seen enough. Shavoth said. As he grabbed Tarah's hand. Jahdson picked up the crystal ball and took it into his room. Well I am going to go for a walk and let my two favorite girls sleep. As he kissed Rosey on the cheek. Nevis said.

Don't leave me. Rosey said.

I promise I won't go far anyway I have to get things ready for our wedding. Nevis said.

Ok I guess I am a little tired.

Nevis put the baby in the crib and walked out of the room.

Now that my child is born I have to make Rosey think everything is going to change for the better but I am still going to do what I set out to do. Nevis said to himself.

Nevis went down and told the knight to give this note to his son Shavoth and do not hurt him this time.

The knight nodded and left towards Elphany's palace.

Then Nevis went to his lab. Well I will get my powers back I just have to find the spell that will reverse what they done.

He went and took his book off the shelf. Read off one of the spells. At that a bouquet of flowers came out.

Well someone has been messing around down here. Well I can fix that and he went into the room off the far wall and grabbed another hook that he had hid in there.

He opened it to the page he had marked and read off one of the spells. At that there was a puff of smoke and a lizard appeared in the room.

Well they didn't find this book. As he reversed the spell and the lizard disappeared.

He went to the page that had giving him the powers and he read them off.

He pointed his finger at the wall and a bolt of lightning went through the air. Now we will see who has the last laugh. Nevis said. As he laughed a wicked laugh.

He went over to where his crystal ball was and it was gone well I guess whoever was in this room has my crystal ball.

I will fix that he went through his book and read off a spell. Now if anyone touches it they will get a shock for stealing it. Wait a minute they seen everything that was going on if I do that then they will know what I am up to. Nevis reversed the spell.

Now that I have my powers it is only a matter of time that things will be going my way. He went and grabbed the other crystal ball and looked in it he seen what everyone at Elphany's was doing he seen the knight hand the note to Shavoth good my plan is working. Now to finish what I have set out to do. It is working better then I thought.

I must go back up to see Rosey before she suspects anything. Nevis said. As he went up to his room the baby started crying.

Ok my little darling I am coming. He heard Rosey talking.

As he walked in the room he had seen Rosey changing the baby. Nevis walked up to her. I see she didn't sleep long at all. Nevis said.

No she will be keeping us up for a while. Rosey said.

The baby started crying again. Well I think she is hungry. Rosey said. Let's go for a ride. Tarah looked at Shavoth.

Yes let's Nevis isn't going to be doing anything for a while anyway. Shavoth said.

They rode out to Remus's cabin. As they got closer. How would you like to build a home out by the cabin? Elphany asked.

It is nice out here and I think Remus would have wanted it that way. Shavoth said.

They climbed off the horses and went in the cabin. I am going to see in can find us something to eat. Shavoth said.

Tarah walked around the cabin remembering when she was growing up in here. There were tears flowing from her eyes.

Shavoth came up to her and wrapped his arms around her. I am so sorry that Remus had to die. I will be ok and kissed him on the lips. Tarah said.

I am going up to take a shower. I have food cooking in the kitchen. Can you check it so it doesn't burn? He asked.

Tarah remembered the fireplace. Went over to it did the same thing that her uncle told her to do. I just wonder if there is anything else in there. She said.

She started tapping on the bricks waited. Nothing was happening as she was about to walk away the brick. slid open.

She looked inside and found a leather bag and pulled it out. There was a piece of paper in there. With a ribbon tied around it.

She untied it and opened the paper and started reading it.

My dearest Tarah,

I know when you get this letter I will be gone. In this bag are things to start your life over again. I just hope and pray that you have stopped Nevis. And you are living a nice peaceful life.

I just wish I was there to see you and your parents reunite.

Just remember I will always love you and hope you will find all the love and happiness that you can. In the bag is a chart. And on it. It will show you how to get to your parents on earth.

Shavoth walked in when she was reading the letter. What is that? He asked.

It is a letter from uncle Remus. She answered.

Did you check the food in the kitchen? He asked.

No I'm sorry I didn't. she answered.

Shavoth walked in the kitchen and checked the food.

Tarah went on reading. In the wall where you got this bag out there is a box take it out and open it. Tarah put the letter down and took the box out and opened it.

There was a lot of papers in it. She took them out and there was just numbers on them one said twenty one said five, ten, fifty and hundred. There were a lot of numbers on it.

She picked the letter back up and it read this is what they call money it was they use on earth. They use it instead of gems. That we use here.

You can take the gems with you and use them to trade for money.

I will always be with you in your heart forever and ever. And I will be watching you from above.

Love always, Remus.

What did the letter say? Shavoth asked. Tarah told him and showed him the paper this is what they call money on earth.

Well it looks like we are in for a lot of changes in our life. Shavoth said.

But what about leaving this planet? This is the only home that I know and I don't know of any other life then this one. Tarah asked.

Shavoth walked over to Tarah and pulled her to him as long as we are together we can go anywhere we want and if going to another planet to live I can do it as long as you are by my side forever. You have my heart my soul and my life in your hands and that will always be my love. He bent his head and gave her a passionate kiss on the lips. Then looked in her eyes and said you are my love and I shall always be by your side.

Can we eat now? The food is ready grabbing Tarah by the hand and leading her to the kitchen.

Nevis wants us to go and watch the wedding. And he wants to get to know me. Shavoth was telling Tarah while they were eating.

Well I guess it wont hurt. And right now he doesn't have his powers back and it will be a while before he can. Tarah said

Ok but I am going to be cautious about him the whole time we are there. And from we have seen he has changed. Shavoth said.

Yes he has but he could be doing it because he knows what Jahdson did to him. Shavoth said. True but lets not go to far into it I still have my powers. Tarah said.

Elphany was sitting next to Joe on the patio. That was their favorite spot to sit when it started getting dark out.

I really am glad to be home. Elphany said.

Yes I am so glad that Nevis has finally gave up on trying to get back at you. Joe said.

Yes but I think the only reason why. He is doing this to Rosey is because he lost his powers and he doesn't want to lose his daughter. Elphany said.

Yes you could be right I guess we have to get prepared cause if he gets his powers back he is going to be worse then he ever was. Joe said.

Joe reached out and put his arm around Elphany. I am so glad we have each other. He said. That is so true I love you so. Elphany said.

And I love you more. Joe said.

After Rosey fed the baby. She looked at Nevis would you like to hold your daughter? Yes I would like that very much. He said.

Rosey handed Katey to him. He was looking at her so small how could I have been so cruel when you were pregnant with Shavoth. I wish I could go back in time and change everything. Nevis said.

Well at least you proved yourself when he comes to our wedding. Rosey said.

Yes that is true and I promise I will be different, if it takes me the rest of our life's to prove it to you. Nevis said.

I hope so cause all I want is you and the children in my life forever. Rosey said. Nevis looked at Rosey. We need to get you ready for our wedding.

We have a week left and I am exhausted right now all I want to do is sleep right now. Rosey said. Nevis put the baby in the crib then went over and hugged and kissed her.

You get your rest and I will get things prepared for our wedding. He told her.

And take revenge at the same time he said to himself.

A few hours later Rosey was up walking around feeling better everyday and she owed it all to Nevis. The love he was showing her was bringing her back to life.

What she didn't know is what Nevis was up to. If she did she would take the baby and leave for good. Shavoth and Tarah rode up to the Nevis's palace. The knight greeted them and took their horses to the stable.

Something doesn't seem right. Tarah said just keep your eyes open. I feel the same way as you do. Shavoth said.

They walked into the palace. The maid greeted them and showed them to their room. Well I guess we have to wait to see what is going to happen. Shavoth said.

About an hour went by and then there was a knock on the door.

Shavoth went to the door and opened it slowly. It was the maid.

Your mother would like to see the both of you.

Shavoth thanked her. Then he and Tarah followed her down the hall. When they got the his mothers room. Shavoth knocked on the door.

Rosey said come in please.

Shavoth opened the door grabbed Tarah by the hand and walked in. Rosey was sitting on the bed holding the baby.

Are you alright mother? Shavoth asked.

Shavoth was looking at Nevis. He still didn't trust him. But what he really wanted to do was pick Nevis up and throw him out the window. But thought otherwise cause he knew his mother was right here.

Its ok Shavoth Nevis has really changed. and he doesn't have his powers anymore. So the both of you don't have anything to worry about. Rosey said.

It is true I have changed and it is all thanks to your mother. Nevis said.

Tarah just stood there she could sense something wasn't right but she didn't want to let Nevis know what she knew and just the way he was acting that it would probably happen real soon. She looked at Shavoth and knew that he could feel it to her hand was starting to hurt from Shavoth squeezing it to hard she wiggled her fingers and he eased up on his grip.

Would you like to see your little sister? Nevis asked. Shavoth walked over to look at the baby.

I am truly sorry for not getting to know you all those years that you were growing up. But if you will let me I will try to show you that I am a changed man. Nevis said.

You can come in to Tarah. Rosey said you are part of the family now. Tarah came in and sat on the edge of the bed.

Rosey and Tarah started talking.

Nevis looked a Shavoth would you like to hold your sister? Nevis asked. Shavoth shook his head yes. And Rosey handed the baby to him.

Again I am really sorry for the grieve that I have caused you. And as for you Nevis was looking at Tarah.

I did love you mother dearly and she was my whole life. I was really hurt when I came back from the war and found her married to someone else. But I shall never be that way again.

I have Rosey to thank for that. Nevis looked at Rosey with such love. How could Tarah and Shavoth not believe him?

Rosey started crying I am so glad you said that Nevis. I love you and she grabbed his hand.

What is her name? Shavoth asked.

Katy Rose is her name. Nevis said. That is a beautiful name. Tarah said. Well it is almost time. Nevis said.

Shavoth handed the baby to Nevis. We will be waiting downstairs for you two downstairs.

At that Shavoth and Tarah walked out the door. Let's go get ready. Shavoth said. As they were getting ready. Do you think that he has really change? Shavoth asked.

I am not sure but something just doesn't feel right. Tarah said.

There was a knock on the door. When Shavoth answered it. It was Nevis.

I am sorry for bothering you but was going to put the wedding off till tomorrow you mother fell asleep after she fed the baby. Could you stay the night? Nevis asked.

Is it ok with you Tarah? Shavoth asked. Yes that will be fine. Tarah said.

Ok well you can go out in the garden if you like. I will have the maid fix you some food. And you can go out in the garden if you like. Nevis said.

I really do love your mother. And I will take good care of her. I hope you can forgive me. Nevis said.

Thank you and I will try to forgive you. Shavoth said.

Tarah just stood there looking at Nevis. Trying to read his face. Ok well I will see you two in the morning then. Nevis said.

Shavoth watched him walk down the hallway. Well he sure is being too nice isn't he? Shavoth said.

Yes and he is up to something but I am not sure what. Tarah said. don't know if we should stay or not. I am getting worried. But if we leave he might hurt my mother. Shavoth said. well then I guess we stay for now. Tarah said.

The maid brought their food to them and they ate most of it. That wasn't too bad. Tarah said.

Well I am really getting tired. Shavoth said.

Lets go to bed. Tarah said. They climbed in bed and in no time they were fast asleep.

The next morning Nevis went downstairs. Rosey was sound asleep yet so he didn't wake her up.

He didn't want to make the maid suspicious so he was ordering her around he asked which try of food was who's?

When she told him he grabbed some flowers and put them on Rosey's tray. Then when the maid turned around he poured some powder in all the drinks. I will take mine and Rosey's up you take the rest.

Rosey was still sleeping Nevis went in and put the tray of food on the table. Then he went over and gave Rosey a kiss on the cheek.

Rosey stirred a little it's time for breakfast.

Nevis said wake up breakfast is here. Soon my dear I shall have what I want and then we will be happy.

What did you say? Rosey asked.

I said it's time to eat. He helped her out of bed and sat her in the chair by the table.

Nevis went over and looked to see if the baby was ok. Are you going to eat with me? Rosey asked.

Yes but I just wanted to look at my baby girl first. Nevis said.

He walked over and sat down at the table and started eating his food.

I am so happy we are getting married. Rosey said.

So am I. Nevis said. He reached out and grabbed Rosey's hand and kissed the back of it.

Rosey grabbed her juice and drank it down. Would you like to go for a walk when you are done eating? Nevis asked.

That would be nice I do need to get out for a while. Rosey said.

Tarah and Shavoth were just waking up when there was a knock on the door. Who is it? Shavoth called out.

It is the maid sir with your breakfast.

Shavoth stood up and put his robe on. Went to the door and let the maid in. She put the tray on the table then left the room.

Tarah got up and walked over to the table and sat down in the chair.

Shavoth joined her. Tarah took a drink out of her juice. When she did she spit across the room.

Don't drink that stuff. I think Nevis put something in it. Tarah said.

He *picked* up the food and the drinks and dumped them in the toilet and flushed the food down.

Well *Nevis* is going to have a big surprise. Shavoth said.

Yes he will but we are going to have to make him think that we are under his spell. Tarah said.

We are going to have to figure out what to do. Now that we know that he is up to something. Shavoth said. And kissed Tarah on the lips.

If Nevis is up to something then it has to be big for him to try to put us to sleep. And I am going to have to stop him. Tarah said.

Not if I get to him first. And if I do I will end up putting him in his grave. Shavoth said.

I just wonder how he is going to do this now that he doesn't have his powers. He can't harm anyone. You can see he does love your mother a lot. Tarah said.

Well he wants you that is for sure. Shavoth said.

We had better get ready he will be in soon. Tarah stood up and walked over to the bed and lie down. Shavoth followed her.

Wait a minute he said. He went over to the tray and knocked the trays on the floor. Let's make it look good. As he climbed in bed. Shavoth said.

I am a little tired right now whatever little bit I *did* drink made me a little tired. Tarah said.

Get a little sleep. I will keep watch. I'll wake you when I hear Nevis coming. Shavoth said. Shavoth looked over Tarah was out cold.

Nevis looked over at the baby and she started stirring someone is hungry so he went *over*. Changed her and handed her to Rosey.

I am going to go check and see if Shavoth and Tarah are up. Nevis said as he kissed Rosey on the cheek.

Wake up Tarah someone is coming. Shavoth said. Shavoth lay there pretending he was asleep.

The door opened slowly and Nevis popped his head in. This is great my plan is going to work perfectly. And he closed the door. Walked back into his room That's what you think. Shavoth said.

Right now I have to get things ready. Nevis said.

He went down to the lab. He picked up the thing that he was working on. Won't everyone be surprised at what I have made. I am going to pay Elphany back for and if anyone tries to stop me they will die.

He started working on the thing he had in his hand.

Upstairs Shavoth was looking out the window while Tarah slept.

What could he be up to right? He and mother will be married soon. Then we will find out what he is up to. Shavoth said.

Shavoth walked over to the bed and looked at Tarah. How beautiful you are. You are my one and only love and I am going to protect you. He bent down and kissed her on the lips.

Tarah opened her eyes. She was still sleepy from the drug. She smiled and said. Hello my beloved husband. So what has happened so far? Tarah asked.

He told her what happened that morning.

There was a knock on the door. Shavoth jumped in bed and they laid there pretending to be asleep.

The maid opened the door and seen that they were asleep so she grabbed the tray and left and went into see if Rosey was finished.

Are Shavoth and Tarah awake yet? Rosey asked.

No they are still sound asleep. The maid said.

Ok thank you. Rosey said.

That's *odd* Shavoth is usually the first one up. Rosey said.

Nevis put the object down that he was working on and went back up to the bedroom. As he walked in the room he went over to see how the baby was. She sure dies sleep a lot. Nevis said.

Well I am going to get myself ready for our wedding Rosey said. I can't wait till we are married. Nevis said.

Elphany and Joe were sitting on the patio. Where are Tarah and Shavoth? Elphany asked I am not sure I haven't seen them since yesterday. Joe answered.

Rosey came back out of the bathroom I think I am going to take a little nap right now I am really tired for some reason. Rosey said.

The minute she laid her head on the pillow she was fast asleep. Nevis went over and kissed her on the cheek.

I do love you so much my dear Rosey but I have to do this. Rosey are you awake? Nevis asked.

Rosey didn't make a sound. Well now she won't have a clue of what I am going to do.

Nevis went over and picked up the baby. Looked at her. You are such a beauty. After I am finished I will raise you up proper. But first I have some unfinished business to take care of.

The baby opened her eyes and looked up at him. The look she gave him was so pure and innocent. Then she closed her eyes and went back to sleep.

He took one more look at Rosey and she was fast asleep.

At that he took the baby down to the lab. As he walked in the lab he walked over to a far wall by the fireplace. Moved one of the bricks and the fireplace slid open. He walked inside and the fireplace slid back to where it was.

77

He took the baby and put her in a basket. Looked at her and said no one will ever take you from me. He covered her up. I will be back to feed you in a little while. Then he turned and left.

He went back up to his room looked in on Rosey. She was sound asleep. He climbed in bed and slept for a few hours.

When he awoke he looked at Rosey she was still sound asleep.

I need to go feed the baby he said to himself. So he went down to the kitchen found what he needed and took it into the baby. He had seen that she was awake so he fed her and held her until she was asleep.

Then he went upstairs and snuck in the bathroom. Rosey is going to wake up any second now.

He stood on the other side of the room adjusted the mirror and watched until Rosey woke up.

Rosey woke up she tried focusing her eyes they were fuzzy from sleeping for so long. Turned over and looked out the window and smiled soon I will be married to Nevis.

I bet you are getting hungry. Rosey looked over at the baby.

As she stood up to walk to the crib the smile fell from her face. And she started screaming.

Nevis sneered at the screaming. As he came running out of the bathroom. What is wrong are you in pain? Nevis asked.

Rosey shook her head back and forth pointed at the crib. Nevis looked down at the crib and the baby was gone.

I will kill the person who took my daughter. Nevis screamed.

He grabbed Rosey's hands I promise you that I will find our baby. I bet Elphany is behind this. Nevis said.

But Elphany isn't around here you had her banned off this planet. Rosey said as she started crying.

No they are back they have been back for a few months now. And I will find her and pay her back for taking our child. Nevis said.

Nevis went out into the hallway and yelled for the maid.

The maid came running into the room. Yes master Nevis. The maid said.

Someone has taken my daughter and I want to know who did it. Find out if Elphany has been around. And bring me Tarah and Shavoth now. Nevis screamed at the maid. The maid took off running to get Tarah and Shavoth.

The maid knocked on the door when thy didn't answer she went inside. Went over to the bed. And woke Shavoth and Tarah up. Master Nevis wants you in his room right now.

Then the maid went down and told the knights what was going on.

The knights went and saddled the horses. And took off towards Elphany's palace. When they were off the grounds one of them looked around to see if anyone else was around.

One of the knights spoke up. I wonder if Nevis had something to do with the baby disappearing.

Yes I was wondering the same thing. He has been trying to get back at Elphany for a long time. And that is why he wants Tarah. The other knight said.

I know but if we don't do as he says he is going to kill us. The first knight said.

Are you thinking what I am thinking they both said at the same time? They kicked the horses and they took off running.

I think it's time that Elphany used her powers to stop Nevis. After a while they slowed the horses down.

I will be so glad when things get back to normal. The first knight said.

Elphany stood up. Reached her hand out to Joe let's go for a walk. Joe stood up and grabbed her hand. They walked around the garden. I wonder where Tarah and Shavoth went? Elphany asked.

They will be back soon. If you can remember when we were first married how many times we went off alone. Joe said.

That's right. But with all that went on this last few weeks I am a little concerned. Elphany said.

Well let's go find Jahdson to see what's going on.

As they walked towards the palace. Joe was saying you know we never talked about this before but I really love it here. With all our friend~ and the how beautiful it is here. But it doesn't feel like home anymore.

I know I feel the same way that you do. I really would like to go back to earth

I feel more at home there. Elphany said.

Well then when things are better here we will go back. Tarah can take care of the palace and stay here. Joe said.

I know but I don't want to leave her again. Elphany said.

Well then we will have to sit down and talk to Tarah and see what she wants to do. Joe said.

And what are we going to tell our friend on earth when we do go back. I just hope they didn't see the space ship. Elphany said.

We can fix that. We can go back to the day before. So no one will know anything. Joe said.

Joe stopped and pulled Elphany to him. You are just as beautiful today as you were the first day we met.

And you are just as handsome as you were the first day we met. Elphany said. Joe be t down and kissed her on the lips.

They walked in the palace and went to find Jahdson. He was up in his room working on a project.

Joe asked him to get the crystal ball.

Jahdson stood up and took the crystal ball off the dresser and looked in it. When he did he said there is trouble over there.

When Elphany and Joe looked in the crystal ball they could see that Nevis was mad and Rosey was sitting on the bed crying.

The baby is gone Elphany said. I bet Nevis had something to do with it. You don't have to guess that one. Joe said.

Oh no there is Tarah and Shavoth standing in the room. Elphany said. We need to get there and help them Joe said.

I am going to. Jahdson said.

No you are not you are staying here this time and you are not going to argue the point. Elphany said.

Elphany and Joe took off out of the room and out to the horses.

Elphany told the gardener to tell Lavasco that they needed his help. And get the rest of the crew together and follow us to Nevis's now.

Elphany and Joe took off down the path out towards Nevis's.

It didn't take Lavasco, Robert, Tripper and the rest of the knights to catch up to Elphany and Joe.

They all were halfway there when they ran into the two knights that Nevis sent to get Elphany.

Elphany reached down to grab her ankle bracelet and it was gone. I lost my bracelet. Elphany said.

Wish for it. Joe said.

Elphany wished for it and it appeared in her hand. She stretched it out and held into a sword and held it out in front of her.

As they approached the knights to fight them.

They knights started yelling we don't want to fight you we want to join you. Well let's go then we have no time to lose.

The knights turned around and took off towards Nevis's.

146

Nevis was yelling at Tarah I want my daughter back I know you two had something to do with it.

What are you talking about? Tarah yelled back.

My daughter is gone and someone has her. Nevis yelled.

Well I don't have her we were in our room all night you know that. Shavoth said. I am sorry mother but I did not take my sister. Shavoth said.

Rosey reached out her hand to Shavoth.

Nevis stopped him no one comes near Rosey until my daughter *is* back in her mother's arms.

And it was either Tarah or Elphany that had something to do with it.

And I will start destroying everything I see until I get my daughter back. Nevis yelled for the knight to come in. when the knight came in Nevis ordered the knight to lock Tarah and Shavoth in their room and they cannot leave until his daughter is found.

The knight ushered them out to their room. And locked the door.

Tarah looked at Shavoth. You know that the only person that took your sister was Nevis. I am going to give up and let him take me. I am tired of fighting. Tarah said.

No your not if you do then he will still destroy everything and everyone.

And if your mom and dad were looking through the crystal ball then they are on their way here. Shavoth said.—

Ok but I am going to stop him once and for all. I am tired of being afraid. Tarah said.

I have to go and help look for Katy Rose. You stay here and get some rest. I promise I will bring her back to you when I find her and then we can get married. Nevis said as he kissed her on the cheek. He went in the bathroom and got a glass of water for Rosey and put some sleeping powder in it.

Her drink this he said.

Rosey drank half of the water. Why is this happening to me? Am I not supposed to be happy? Rosey asked. She lie down and fell fast asleep.

Nevis went down to the lab, went into the secret room behind the fireplace the baby was crying. I am so sorry little one as he picked her up and held her. Went over and fixed a bottle and fed her.

I promise you everything will be just fine real soon. Nevis said.

When the baby was done eating he changed her and laid her back in the crib. Then he went in the lab finished the project he was working on. I have only one shot with this and it had better work. Nevis said.

Elphany and everyone showed up at Nevis's.

Be cautious Nevis could have his powers back Elphany said. They jumped off the horses and ran into the palace.

Elphany ran up to Nevis's bedroom and ran in. Rosey was lying on the bed sleeping.

Check all the other rooms Elphany ordered one of the knights.

When she ran down the hall she seen one of the knights standing in front of the room that Tarah and Shavoth were in. Elphany held her sword out either open the door or you die.

The knight didn't argue he opened the door. Let's go Elphany yelled at Tarah and Shavoth.

They came running out and followed Elphany down the hall Elphany looked at the knight leave and don't come back, The knight took off running out of the palace.

Elphany said I am going to find Nevis and stop him once and for all. I am going with you Tarah said.

No! This is between me and Nevis now go home and wait for me there. Elphany ordered Tarah. And tell everyone to go with you.

Tarah left with Shavoth and went to find the rest of them. She told them what Elphany said.

We are not leaving without her Joe said. I am going to help her. She is my wife. And Joe took off to look for Elphany.

Tarah looked at Shavoth I have to help my parents. I cannot let them fight Nevis alone.

Wait Tarah Shavoth said. There is something I have to tell you.

Your uncle told me that when the time comes that you do have to fight Nevis it has to be you and your mother together to stop him. Shavoth said.

But how do I do that? Tarah asked.

All Remus said were you and your mother would know what to do.

All right let's go find were they are. We don't have much time. And you can find your sister and take her to your mother then take her to our home. Tarah said. They ran in the palace and went looking for Elphany.

They looked allover the palace ran in the kitchen found the maid Shavoth told the maid to go up to and stay with Rosey. And don't leave the room for any reason at all.

The maid did as Shavoth said.

They must be in the lab. As they went in there please get my father out of here and take him home with you if you have to knock him out do it. Tarah said.

We are all leaving together. Shavoth said.

When they walked in the lab. Nevis had a knife to Joe's neck. Elphany was ordering Nevis to let Joe go.

When Tarah seen they I wish for daddy to stand by me. Joe was standing next to his daughter.

Do you think that will stop me from getting what I want? Nevis yelled. Where's my baby sister? Shavoth yelled.

That you will never find out. I never wanted you in the first place and you will never see your sister again. Nevis yelled.

Shavoth just looked at Nevis he held back the tears. Kill that man I don't have a father. Shavoth said.

I am not going to kill him I am going to make him wish he was dead. Go find your sister. Tarah said.

Lavasco and the rest of them came running in find the baby. Elphany yelled. They all took off to find the baby. Joe please go with them Tarah and I will take care of Nevis.

Do you think that the two of you can stop me from getting what I want? Nevis yelled and laughed a wicked laugh.

Yes we do Elphany and Tarah said at the same time.

Nevis pointed his finger at Tarah. When he did Tarah started rising up in the air.

Put her down. Elphany yelled.

As you wish. Nevis said. And he raised his hand higher and waved his hand and Tarah flew across the room and hit the wall.

Elphany ran over to Tarah, bent down are you ok? Elphany asked. Yes he just knocked the wind out of me that's all. Tarah said.

Elphany stood up real slow and turned around do you think that I will let you take our powers away? That's one thing that is sacred and I will not let you have it to use for your evil purposes. Elphany said as she started walking towards *Nevis.*

Nevis started to raise his hand towards Elphany. Elphany jumped and did a flip in the air.

You are going to have to do better than that. Elphany said.

Nevis shot a bolt of lightning through the air at Elphany. This time Elphany flipped towards the right.

Then she did three flips and with the last flip she kicked Nevis in the mouth. Did you forget that I am still as strong and fast as I used to be? Give it up you cant win. Elphany said.

Tarah stood up and ran up to Nevis.

And I am here to help her. Tarah said.

Nevis looked at Tarah then at Elphany holding his mouth.

He slipped through them, ran to the table grabbed the object he was working on. Wrapped his cape around him and disappeared out of the lab.

We have to find him and stop him now. Elphany said.

What a minute. I hear something. Tarah said.

They listened for a minute. I don't hear anything. Elphany said. Then there was a faint cry. Do you hear it now? Tarah asked.

It's in here somewhere. They walk around the room. There's got to be a hiding wall somewhere here. Elphany said.

They started tapping on the fireplace when the fireplace opened up. When they looked in the room there was the baby in there crying.

Tarah ran in and picked the baby up. Your safe now. Tarah said holding the baby close.

Let's get her out of here. Before Nevis comes back. Elphany said. They took the baby to out and went to find the rest of them.

Shavoth was out on the terrace. Tarah took the baby to him here is your sister. Tarah said. As she handed the baby to him. Go get your mother and the rest of the men and take them home.

Did you stop Nevis? Shavoth asked.

No not yet he disappeared on us again. But were going after him now. Tarah said. Get them out of here now. Tarah said. She hugged Shavoth and her and Elphany took off.

Shavoth took the baby up to Rosey. Rosey was sound asleep on the bed.

The maid was in the chair. Shavoth looked at the maid get my mother ready. You and my mother are going with me. Don't worry about bringing anything. Just wake my mother up. Shavoth said.

When the maid couldn't wake Rosey Shavoth handed the baby to the maid and picked Rosey up off the bed. Let's go. Shavoth said.

They walked out of the room and down the stairs. As they started to go out the door. Nevis was standing there you are not taking Rosey and my daughter anywhere. Nevis yelled.

How are *you* going to stop me? Shavoth asked.

I will kill you before you leave this place. Nevis laughed an evil laugh. Lavasco and everyone walked in. we will stop you Nevis. Lavasco said. Then Elphany and Tarah walked in. Tarah went over and opened the door.

Go get out of here everyone. They all started running out the door.

Nevis followed.

I said you weren't taking them with you. Nevis yelled.

Shavoth kept walking. Went out to the carriage house and put his mother in the carriage. Then helped the maid in with the baby. He tied a team of horses on the carriage and took off. Joe, Lavasco and the rest of them followed him off the grounds towards Elphany's palace.

Nevis ran out to try to stop them he shot a bolt of lightning out of his finger. Hit on of the knights and the knight and the horse was nothing but powder.

Nevis was about to shoot another bolt of lightning aiming at Joe when Elphany raised her foot up and kicked him in the hand.

That will be the last time that you will destroy anyone. Elphany said. The bolt of lightning went up in the air.

Nevis grabbed his hand as he yelled in pain. You did it to me again didn't you? You left me then you take them away from me. Nevis· screamed at Elphany.

You did it to yourself. Elphany yelled back.

I am going to take both you and Tarah's powers now.

You really think it is that easy to take our powers away? Tarah said.

Yes I do my plan worked out just as I wanted it to if not better. Nevis said.

Shavoth looked behind him everyone was with him but one of the knights, which Nevis killed.

He stopped the team of horses. Climbed off went back to check on his mother and sister. His sister was fast asleep but his mother was starting to wake up. What's going on? Rosey demand as she looked around. When she seen the baby she took her out of the maids arms. Oh my little baby girl you are back. And started kissing the baby.

What's going on Shavoth? Rosey asked.

I am so sorry mother. Nevis took the baby and hid her. He hasn't changed at all. He even told me that he never wanted me. Shavoth started crying.

Well we are never going back there again. I promise you that. Rosey said. I am so glad to hear that. Shavoth said.

Joe and the rest of them caught up to Shavoth. Is everything ok? Joe asked. Yes everything is better then ever. Rosey said.

Well you are going to come home with us and stay at the palace. Joe said. Yeas you are and I will take care of you. Lavasco said. As he climbed off his horse and walked over to the carriage. May I ride with you? Lavasco asked. You are more then welcome to sit in here with us. Rosey said.

Lavasco climbed in and sat down across from Rosey. May I hold the baby? Lavasco asked.

Yes you can hold her anytime you want. Rosey said. Let's get going I am getting hungry. Lavasco said.

I am worried about Elphany and Tarah. I am going back. Joe said.

No you can't if you do then you could get killed. Anyway if Tarah and Elphany work together they will defeat him and if you are there and he kills you Elphany will let him take her. So let's just go home and wait. Lavasco said.

Joe was hesitant but he knew that Lavasco was right.

They took off for the palace.

CHAPTER 9

What makes you think that you can take our powers without killing us? Do you really want to kill us? Elphany asked.

If that what it takes. I will. Nevis said.

You have taking everything that I ever loved away from me. I have nothing left But to take the powers that you and Tarah have. And I am going to do that now.

Oh no *your* not Tarah flipped in the air and landed on top of Nevis knocking him on the ground.

Now who is going to stop whom? Tarah asked.

Nevis started screaming get off of me now *you* fool.

Tarah started punching Nevis in the face you will never take our powers from us. Nevis wasn't saying anything. Elphany said stop Tarah. He's not moving.

Elphany checked his pulse well he still alive you just knocked him out.

Tarah got up I am going to find some rope to tie him up and walked out towards the stable. She found the rope and came back. Nevis was just waking up his face was swelled and he could barely see out' of his eyes. YOU did a number on him. Elphany said.

Well that will teach him for messing with us, Tarah said. she started tying with the ropes, What are you doing to me. Nevis yelled.

Doing what I should of done a long time ago. So I can knock some sense in that thick skull of yours. Elphany said.

You can say what ever you want that isn't going to change the way I feel. Owe that's to tight you idiot. Nevis; said.

Tarah put her finger in the rope. Looked up at Nevis. did yell think I was going to fall for that one. Tarah said. Now maybe you can talk some sense into him. Tarah said. She started walking away

Where are you going? Elphany asked.

To get a drink. Would you like on to? Tarah. asked yes I would and bring Nevis something to. Elphany said.

Tarah left to get some drinks.

Don't bother I will be fine Soon. Nevis said. We will see about that. Elphany said as she sat down on the grass. Will you listen to me now? She asked. Do I have a choice not to? Nevis said.

She ignored what he just said. When you went off to war I begged you not to go.

And you went anyway. I was heartbroken when you were gone for so long a few men had came back a few years later and said you were dead, it took me a long time to come to terms of your death.

I went on with my life, I loved you so much. Elphany said.

But I was in the hospital with head wounds and lost my memory due to the head wounds. Until right before I came back. Nevis said.

You wouldn't even let me explain at all why I married Joe he was a good friend of the both of us.

When you asked him to watch over me when you left. I waited for so long for you to return. Joe was such a good friend and always there-to console me when. I was upset when we heard the news of your death.

I grieved for so long I wanted so bad to die to be with you.

And then one day I fell in love with Joe I don't know how it happened it just did. And I still do love you but my life is with Joe now and yours is with Rosey. Elphany said.

Yes but why didn't you wait just a little longer? When I got my memory back thinking of you all the time is what kept me alive. Why didn't you just stab me in the heart? that's how I felt. Nevis said he bowed his head and started crying.

Please forgive me. And lets go on with our life's as they are. You have a new baby.

And a woman that loves you. And I know that you love her. Shavoth would love to get to know you. And I know you didn't mean what you said to him. Elphany said.

No I didn't but I don't think he is ever going to forgive me this time and I wouldn't blame him at all. Nevis said. Tarah walked back with pitcher of juice and three glasses. One of them she put some sleeping powder in and held it far enough away so Nevis wouldn't see it.

I think that Shavoth would forgive you if you go to him and talk to him. Let him know what is in your heart. Its going to take some time to earn his trust. Tarah said.

Yes you are right. I should have listened to you years ago. Then things wouldn't have gotten out of control. And started crying again boy that really hurts. Nevis said.

Well you haven't cried in years have you? Elphany asked.

I have made so many mistakes over he years. How will I ever make it up to everyone. I feel really bad. Nevis said.

He was doing everything to make them believe that he had changed.

Well first thing you need to do is to go back and apologize to Rosey. Then work on everyone else. Tarah said.

Well I can't do it with my hands tied now can I? Nevis said. Would you like a drink? Tarah asked. She poured Nevis a drink.

Yes I would please. Nevis said. Tarah put the glass to his mouth and gave him a drink. No you can't but can we trust you to be the person you once was? Elphany asked.

Do you remember all the wonderful things we used to do together? Nevis asked.

Yes I do and you were a wonderful person then. Elphany said. And I can be again.

Now that I know why you fell in love and married someone else. I would have done the same thing if you would have died. And I am such a fool. Rosey stayed no matter how mean I was to her. I have a lot of making up to do. Nevis said.

Well what do you think? Elphany looked at Tarah.

I don't know. Tarah said.

Oh please I cannot prove that I have changed being tied up like this. Nevis put his chin down on his chest and he started crying.

Well I guess we can untie him. Tarah said as she stood up and went to untie him. After she did he stood up I am really truly sorry for all the pain I have caused you in your life and I will try to make up to you. Nevis said.

That's all I ask for. Elphany said.

Well we must go home. We will give you time to get yourself in order. Then we will try to send Rosey back to you but you have to prove to her that you will never do anything to hurt her again. Tarah said.

I will prove to you and everyone else that it will be different here from this day on. Nevis said.

Elphany and Tarah stood up and went to get their horses. When they started riding off they yelled back. At the same time they *said* we will be watching every move you make to make sure you are not lying. And they took off.

Nevis was standing there watching them. And we will see if I change. Turned around and laughed an evil laugh. But now I must keep let everyone think that I am going to change. And he walked in the palace.

When Shavoth and everyone else made it home. He helped his mother out of the carriage and walked her in the house. He asked the butler if he could get things for the baby. And show his mother and the maid to a room.

The butler did and Rosey and the maid followed. Rosey looked at Shavoth with such sad eyes.

Don't worry mother things will get better? She just walked away without saying a word.

I hate my father for what he has done to my mother. Shavoth said.

Joe came up and put his hand on Shavoth shoulder. Hopefully Elphany got to Nevis and your mother can go back to him.

Never I will not let him hurt her again. Shavoth said.

I understand. Let's go see how they are doing. Joe said. Lavasco followed them up to Jahdson room.

Jahdson was looking through the crystal ball. He looked behind him to see who walked in. you just missed the pounding that Tarah gave Nevis.

After they had seen everything that went on. Well maybe Elphany got through to Nevis. That's the first time he has ever cried in his life. Lavasco said. Maybe he is going to change. Joe said.

Well maybe but I still don't trust him. Shavoth said.

Yes I know but if he does your mother will go back to him. Joe said.

I know but right now I am really concerned about her. She is really unhappy. Shavoth said.

Well go sit with her then she needs you now. But don't a=say anything until we know for sure. Joe said.

After they seen Elphany and Tarah climb on the horses they left. And went to get cleaned up.

Wait dad can I talk to you. Jahdson asked. What is it son? Joe asked.

I'm scared. I want to go home. I really miss my friends. There is no one here my age to get to know. Jahdson said.

We haven't been here that long for you to find anyone your age to play with. Joe said.

I don't like what is going on here. Nevis is so mean. Jahdson said.

Well you seen that your mother has finally gotten through to him. So things are going to be getting better. Once you get to know this place you will like being here. Just give it some time. And if you still feel the same. We will get everyone together and talk. Joe said.

Ok I will try. Can I go and see what is like outside of the palace? Jahdson asked.

I will ask Lavasco to take you out to see the land. I am going to get cleaned up now. Joe said.

Joe left the room. Jahdson sat there by himself. I have a strong feeling that things are not going to get any better they are going to get worse. Jahdson said.

Elphany and Tarah were on their way home. Do you think I got through to him? Elphany asked.

I am not sure. But he did seem to be sincere about the things he was saying. Tarah said.

Well we will just have to wait and see what happens. Elphany said. Let's get home I am getting hungry and I need a bath. Tarah said. I'll race you Elphany *said.*

They made the horses run within no time they were home jumped off the horses and ran inside.

They were both laughing. Well it's about time there is some happiness in this house. Lavasco said.

Yes I agree with you. What makes me so happy is that we are all together. And this time it is going to stay that way. Elphany said.

I am going to take Jahdson out to show him the land and to see if we can find him some friends to hang around with. Lavasco said.

Ok but don't stay gone long. Joe and I want to talk to everyone. Elphany said. Ok we will be back by dark. Lavasco said.

Let's go Jahdson. Lavasco said.

Have fun son. Elphany said.

Ok love you mom. Jahdson said. And gave her a hug. Bye Tarah. Then Lavasco and Jahdson walked out the door.

Tarah and Elphany went upstairs to take a shower. Nevis was *in* the lab looking through the crystal ball. If you think things are going to be ok think again. I will get what I want and that will be soon. He walked over to the object that he was working on, picked it up and started pushing buttons. I will set this for a six days from now that will give me plenty of time to get Rosey and my daughter back. Then I will get Elphany and Tarah together to get what I need from them.

Then he went out to the kitchen and grabbed as much food as he could took it out to the spaceship and placed the food in the kitchen of the spaceship. Then went out to the engine room to see if there was enough fuel to get where he needed to go.

Ok now I have to make sure that I am not over powered again this time. Nevis said.

Then he walked out to the garden picked the flowers that he thought that Rosey would like. Then he walked in the lab grabbed the object and went out to the stable.

Mounted up the horse and buggy and headed towards Elphany's palace. I have to be really good at this to get them back home. Nevis said.

When he was halfway to Elphany's he stopped the horses looked all around him to see if anyone was there. When he saw that the coast was clear he climbed down and went into the forest dug a hole deep enough to plant the object then buried it. Covered it up and put a rock over top of it. Made it look as if no one had moved the soil went to the creek and washed his hands off. He went back and climbed on the buggy and took off.

When he made it to Elphany's he was met by a lot of people. What are you doing here? Tripper asked.

I come to apologize for all the rotten things I have done in the past and I am asking you if you would like to come and work for me. I promise things will be different.

I like it here just the same. I have no intentions on working for you ever again. Tripper said.

Well if that's the way you feel then I will not argue the point with you.

I am sorry for the way I treated you and I am really sorry for what I did to you. Nevis said.

Can I please see Rosey and my children? Nevis asked.

That's not up to me that's up to them. If I was them I would never have anything to do with you again. Tripper said.

He motioned one of the knights to go get Rosey, Shavoth and the baby. You may wait here. Tripper said.

The knight went in to find Shavoth. He was in the room with his mother and sister.

The knight called Shavoth out of the room and told him what was going on. Ok thanks I will talk to mother and see what she wants to do.

Shavoth went back in the room and sat down in the chair next to his mother.

Mom I have to tell you something. Will you please think about this before we go outside? Nevis out there wants to see all of us. The knight says that he doesn't seem to be a threat but I am not sure about this.

Well I will go talk to him if you go with me. Rosey said.

That's fine with me I wouldn't leave you aloe with him right now if you asked me to. Shavoth said.

Rosey asked the maid to watch the baby as they walked out to talk to Nevis. As they got closer Rosey seen Nevis's face. What happened to him? Rosy asked. Oh Tarah just beat some sense into him that's all. Shavoth said.

Well it has been a long time coming. Rosey said. when they came out to where Nevis was. What is that you want? Rosey asked. Nevis climbed off the buggy.

Rosey and Shavoth backed up a little.

Nevis started to reach in the buggy. Shavoth pulled out his sword.

I am not here to hurt anyone especially the two of you. Nevis said as he grabbed the flowers out of the buggy. These are for you Rosey.

Please forgive me I am so sorry for doing what I did. It took Elphany and Tarah to beat it out of to make me realize that I was wrong. Nevis said.

How are we supposed to believe you with all the hateful things that you have done. I could never trust you again it is over for good this time. You got what you wanted you will never see me or your children again. Rosey said.

Please don't say that. Nevis handed Rosey the flowers.

Rosey threw them on the ground I will never accept anything from you again. She took the ring off her finger and threw it at him. I don't want you in my life again. Let's go Rosey started to turn around to leave.

Nevis started crying please Rosey you and the children are all I need in my life I have come to terms with Elphany and I will not do anything to anyone ever again. I know you can't believe me now but this is coming from my heart I will never do anything to hurt you again. I shall die if you don't come home to me. Nevis put his hands on his eyes and started crying. I am sorry for what I said to you Shavoth I should have never said that I do love you. Nevis said.

I will leave I am really truly sorry for all the hurt I have caused for everyone. Nevis said.

He climbed up on the buggy and started to leave. Then he stopped. Looked at Rosey then Shavoth. Please forgive me for all the hurt I have caused. Then took off.

Shavoth looked at Rosey. Do you really truly love him? Shavoth asked.

With all my heart. I have always loved him. My life isn't complete without him. Rosey said.

Wait Nevis. Shavoth yelled.

Nevis stopped as Shavoth ran up to the buggy. Are you being sincere with my mother? I don't care about our relationship but I do care about my mother and her happiness. Shavoth said.

Nevis climbed off the buggy with all my heart I love her and need her and my children. Nevis said.

Then go to her but if your ever do anything like this to here again I swear I will kill you with my bare hands. Shavoth said.

Oh thank you so much as he hugged Shavoth. Shavoth pulled away from him don't ever touch me again. Shavoth said.

I am sorry Nevis said. I will not do that again.

Nevis took off to Rosey grabbed her and picked her up in his arms and kissed her on the lips.

I will never let you down again. I will always make you happy. There will never be any sorrow in your life again. Nevis said.

Oh Nevis I do love you so but how am I to know that you won't do this to me again. Rosey said.

Because I came here to get you and I did not start a fight with anyone here. I just want you back in my life. He put the ring back on her finger. I want you as my wife. And live with me for the rest of our lives. Nevis said.

I will come back on one condition. That I can leave anytime I want. Rosey said.

I have no problem with that at all you are free to do whatever you want. Nevis said. He sat her down on the buggy seat.

Shavoth ordered the knight to go get the maid and the baby as he walked over to the buggy. Is this what you really want mother? Shavoth asked.

More then anything in the universe. Rosey said.

All I want is for you to be happy. Shavoth said.

The maid came out with the baby and climbed in the buggy.

Let's go home Rosey looked at Nevis. At that they took off. Well I guess maybe he has changed for the better. Shavoth said.

Shavoth Nevis yelled you are more then welcome to come see us anytime you want.

I will do that. Shavoth yelled back.

Then Nevis and Rosey were gone.

Shavoth walked back up to the palace as he started to open the door Tarah beat him to it.

What are you doing out here? Tarah asked.

Letting my mother go back where she needs to be. If she wouldn't have left she would have died without him. She loves him so much. Shavoth said.

I just hope he has changed for your mother's sake. Tarah said.

Me to. He seems sincere. Shavoth said.

It was starting to get dark and Lavasco and Jahdson wasn't back yet I wonder where they are? Elphany asked.

They will be back. Is everyone going to be here? Joe asked. They should be. Elphany said.

Tarah and Shavoth walked in along with all the rest of them.

Lavasco and Jahdson made it back right before the sun went all the way down. How was your day out? Joe asked.

It was all right. Jahdson said.

Now that everyone is here we have something to say to all of you. Elphany said. Joe and I were talking the other day and we were talking about going back to earth. What does everyone think about us leaving? Elphany asked.

If that's what makes you happy then that's what you need to do. But I will miss you so much. Lavasco said.

Well we have room for all of you to come with us. Joe said.

So if you all want to come with us you are all more then welcome to join us. Joe said.

We all might have to go back to earth. Jahdson said. Why do you say that? Tarah asked.

Because that thing that Nevis was working on was a bomb of some kind. Jahdson said.

But he promised my mother that he has changed. Shavoth said. Well we will have to see what happens. Joe said.

Elphany looked at the maids fill the spaceship up with everything that we need.

Elphany said.

The maids shook their heads then went to do as Elphany said.

Lavasco looked really sad. I really don't want to leave my home. But I don't want to lose my friends. Lavasco said.

Well then come with us. You all have a six days. So whoever decides that that they want to go is more then welcome? Elphany asked.

Well I have already decided if it is ok with you Shavoth. Tarah said. I will go wherever you go. Shavoth said.

Then we have a few of you coming with us. I want everyone that is going out at the ship by midday in six days. Elphany said.

Joe and Elphany stood up. Goodnight everyone we will see you in the morning. Let's go in the vault and take all the gems. We will split it up with Tarah and Shavoth. Joe said.

Tarah, Shavoth and Jahdson will you come with us? Elphany asked. You can come to Lavasco if you like.

They all followed Elphany and Joe into the vault. Elphany too the key out of her locket and opened the door. It had been closed for a few years. There was a musty odor coming out. Elphany walked in come on in everyone. Elphany said.

This is beautiful. Lavasco said looking around.

I have some of these that my parents gave me. Lavasco said. He reached in his bag and poured out a handful of gems some of them fell on the floor.

Jahdson bent down and picked the ones up that fell on the floor.

Keep them. Lavasco said.

Well I see that you are almost prepared if you decide to go with us. Elphany said.

Elphany grabbed big suede bag and filled it up with different colored gems. And handed it to Lavasco this is for you. Whether you go with us or not this is my gift to you. I want all of you to grab all the bags you can and fill them up we are going to take all of these with us.

Elphany grabbed some small bags and filled them up. There was about ten of them. These are for the people that don't want to go with us. Elphany said.

Yes we have a lot of loyal people with us. Joe said.

After all the bags were filled. They all looked around. What about the little statues and gold pieces there. Tarah asked.

If you want to take them you are more then welcome. Elphany said. I did leave them to you if I didn't make it back. Elphany said.

The butler came in with a few of the men they were pulling carts behind them.

I thought you might need some help. I have decided to go with you. The men here were wondering if they could bring their family with them. The butler said.

I wouldn't have it any other way. We have room for a thousand people on our spaceship and if we have to we have another spaceship if we don't have room in ours. Joe said.

Can you go out with the butler and get the other one in working order Jahdson? And do you think you can fly it? Elphany asked.

I would be more then happy to do that. And I would love to fly it. Jahdson said. Ok when you have it ready come get me and I will give you a few instructions of how to fly it. Elphany said.

And put some fresh supplies on it and take three of those big bags of jewels and split them up into these small bags and give them to everyone that is going on board. Get some men to help. Then I need a few to spread the word through out the land of our departure. The ones that don't want to go give them a handful of jewels to live on. Joe said.

Mommy I don't know if I really want to go this is the only home that I know. Tarah said.

You will love it there. And if you don't want to stay you can always come back here. Joe said.

What life do we have here? Shavoth asked. Your right and Tarah hugged Shavoth.

Is that all you want to take. Is there anything you would like to grab Jahdson? Elphany asked.

Jahdson looked around. All I want is my family and to go back home. Jahdson. Well then let's get things ready to go. As far as clothes there are stores there that we can buy things so just take a few outfits with you. And spread the word to everyone else. Elphany looked at the butler. Elphany said.

Nevis was looking at Rosey I am so glad that you are with me. I would die without you. You are my life. Nevis said.

As you are my life I cant see myself with no one other then you. Rosey said. Then we shall go find a preacher to marry us right now. And Nevis went to the minister's home. Nevis stopped the buggy in front of the house of god. Went inside and asked the minister if he would marry them. The minister was more then happy to do that.

Can we do it outside? Nevis asked. Yes you may. The minister said.

The minister married them and Nevis gave the minister a few gems. And then they left to go home.

I hope this will prove to you that I have changed and you are the one that I want. Nevis *said.*

This is a start but I am still afraid that you are still going to get your revenge on Elphany. Rosey said.

That is in the past we are starting a whole new life together and from this day on I will be a more kind loving person. Nevis said.

I am so glad to here that. I want to be your friend, lover, wife and mother of your children. I want to have more baby's as many as I can have. Rosey said. That would be so nice to have a houseful of children. Nevis said.

They pulled up in front of the palace. Nevis climbed down off the buggy and picked Rosey up off the seat and carried inside. This is your home to now you are free to go wherever you want. But please promise me you will never leave me. Nevis said.

I promise you I will never leave as long as you are not going back to be that horrible person you were. Rosey said.

You have a deal my beautiful wife. Nevis said.

Nevis looked at the *maid* you are free to stay our leave. I would like it if you stayed to help Rosey with the baby and keep order in the palace. Nevis said.

I would be happy to serve the both of you. The maid said.

Will you go and have the gardener water and feed the horses.

The maid handed the baby to Rosey and went outside.

Well let's get the baby to bed and go to bed ourselves. I have had a long day. Rosey said.

They went up to the bedroom. Put the baby in bed. Rosey went in to take a bath and Nevis sat out and kept an eye on the baby. I have a few days to do what I am going to do. How am I going to convince Rosey to leave this planet? Nevis said.

He sat there thinking for a while I know I have the perfect thing to do to convince her. Nevis said.

Who are you talking to? Rosey asked.

The baby she woke up so I am changing her. She is so beautiful. Nevis said. That was a close one. At least she didn't hear what I was saying. Nevis said. The baby woke up and started crying. Nevis changed her and picked her up. The baby was still crying. I think she is hungry Rosey.

Ok I am almost done here. Rosey said.

Rosey came out of the bathroom in a beautiful white nightgown. Nevis whistled at her you are so beautiful.

Thank you and you are a very handsome man. Rosey said.

The baby was still crying Rosey took the baby and fed her. Why don't you get cleaned up yourself while I feed the baby? Rosey asked.

Nevis went in the bathroom and Rosey fed the baby. The baby fell asleep eating and Rosey put her to bed.

Nevis came out of the bathroom with the towel wrapped around him. He grabbed Rosey picked up and carried her to the bed.

He was so gentle when he made love to her. That she fell more in love with him.

I love you more now then I did before. Nevis said.

And I love you with every beat of my heart. Rosey said.

I am so tired Rosey said.

Well you get some sleep then. Nevis said and kissed her on the forehead. Nevis lay there awake for a while making sure that Rosey was sound asleep.

Then he got out of bed put his robe and slippers on and went down to the lab. He grabs his book of spells. Went through it. Found what he was looking for.

He called it up. Then he ran upstairs with the book in his hands. He put the book in the dresser drawer and climbed in bed.

About five minutes went by and all of a sudden the palace started shaking. Rosey woke up scared what's going on? Rosey asked. The baby she yelled.

Nevis climbed out of bed and grabbed the baby and handed her to Rosey then he sat down beside her. And held her.

The palace shook again. And things falling off the dresser. What is going on Nevis? Rosey asked. Her voice shaking.

I was afraid of this. Nevis said.

What were you afraid of? Rosey asked holding the baby tight so she wouldn't drop her.

That this planet is falling apart. We might have to find another planet to live on. If this keeps happening. Nevis said.

But I don't want to leave my home. I love it here. Rosey said.

Yes but if this planet is falling apart I want to take you someplace safe. And as long as we are together that's all that matters. Nevis said.

The palace shook again. Your right. Rosey said.

Then everything was calm. Maybe that's the only time it will happen. Nevis said. I hope so. Rosey said.

I am going to put the baby back to bed and go back to sleep. Rosey said.

That sounds like a good idea. Nevis said.

They slept until early morn when the baby awoke.

Elphany was giving everyone instructions of what she wanted to take.

Jahdson was excited on going back home. Are we going to live in the same house or find a different home to live in? We have all these jewels to get a palace like this one? Jahdson said.

Your right we can get a big home. Elphany said.

But how are we going to explain this to everyone? Joe asked.

Everyone thought about it for a while. Then Joe said we will have to tell everyone that it is an inheritance.

That's a good idea. Elphany said.

Well I think we have everything that we need now. Tarah said.

Jahdson and the butler went out to work on the spaceship. The butler opened a panel on the outside of the spaceship. There were three buttons on there a blue green and yellow one. He pushed the blue button. The butler pulled Jahdson back a few feet and a door opened. They waited a few minutes then went In. boy this is almost as big as the other one. Jahdson said. I get to fly this one.

They went down to the engine room. The butler tightened up a few things. Then want to see if there was enough fuel on the ship. When he was done. Let's go see if it will start. The butler said. They went in to the front of the spaceship and the butler sat in the captain's chair. Here this is how you start it. Jahdson stood there and watched the butler push some buttons. At that the ship started making a whirring noise. Then stopped. He tried again a few more times and it finally started. It hasn't been in use for a long time but at least its running good now. The butler said.

When you get close to earth you press this button and it makes the spaceship invisible. The butler said.

Ok that will work. Jahdson said. Let's go see if we can help do anything to help your parents. The butler said.

They left the ship. And went towards the palace.

The butler told the men what to put on the ship. And they went to do what he said.

Then the butler and Jahdson into the palace.

Are you going to ride on the spaceship with me? Jahdson asked the butler.

If you want me to. The butler said.

CHAPTER 10

Nevis was sitting there with Rosey eating breakfast. Well what planet would we live on if we have to leave here? Rosey asked

Well what planet would we live on? Rosey asked.

Well the is called earth. Nevis said.

Is it beautiful there? Rosey asked.

Not as beautiful as it is here but it is beautiful. Nevis said.

You know I would follow you wherever you go. Rosey said. and you know I will follow you anywhere. Nevis said. Rosey took Nevis's hand and kissed the back of it. I love you so much. Rosey said. As a tear fell from her right eye.

Nevis stood up and went over and kissed Rosey on the lips. I will be back in a few minutes. Nevis said.

Were are you going? Rosey asked.

Its a surprise that I made for you. And kissed her again. Nevis said. Then he walked into the palace went down to the library. Opened the door and went inside. At the back of the room was a huge door.

He took the key from the hook above the door and went inside lit a candle. Looked around the room. This is all we need to start over. He grabbed some leather bags and filled them as full as he could get them. Then tied the bags. These are so beautiful. They were different colored gems.

Tied the bags up and carried them out to the ship. Oh I forgot something he went back in looked around this is perfect. It was a statue of two people.

He waved his hand around and changed the statue into look a likes of him and Rosey. Then he locked the door and went out to the spaceship put the bags in the spaceship and went back up to Rosey.

170

He hid the statue behind his back. Hello my dear wife as he kissed her on the cheek. Then held the statue out in front of him. Nevis said.

Oh it is so beautiful. Rosey said. As she took it from him.

I am glad you like it. Nevis said.

The baby woke up right about that time. Well I will let you feed our daughter and I will go down for a walk. Nevis said.

All right I am going to go take a nap. When I get done with the baby. Rosey said.

Why don't you come downstairs into the garden later? Nevis asked. Ok I will do that. Rosey said.

Nevis left and went down to the lab. I need to take some things with me when we leave. There is only one more day until I destroy this planet.

He went and grabbed a book of spells out of the backroom he read one of the spells off. Now I will be able to have my powers on earth. Nevis said.

He packed up everything he needed and took it out to the spaceship. Well we have everything that we need now. Nevis said.

When the men came back they told Elphany that there was a lot of people that wanted to go with. About fifteen hundred people.

Did you tell them when we were leaving? Elphany asked. Yes we did on of them answered.

All right if you are going you better get ready. Elphany told them. They left and went to get ready to leave.

Well is everyone here ready to go? Elphany looked around at everyone that was at the dining room table.

What about Succoth? I promised him I would take him with me. Tarah asked. Well I guess he will have to go with us then. Joe said.

Great I guess we are all ready then. Tarah said.

Nevis went out to the garden to meet Rosey. Before he reached the garden he said the spell that he did the night before. With another spell on top of it.

All at once the ground started shaking. Statues started falling on the ground and breaking into pieces. And holes started opening up in the ground.

Rosey came running into the garden with the baby. Oh Nevis it's getting worse. I am scared that someone is going to get hurt. Rosy said.

Don't worry I will protect you. Nevis said. He wrapped his arms around Rosey and the baby.

Then as it began the storm stopped. Well I guess that's all for now. Nevis said. I hope so. I don't like what's going on at all. Rosey said.

They looked around and seen that the palace was starting to fall into ruins. I need to go inside and check on the maid. You will be safe out here. Nevis said.

The gardener came running up to Nevis and Rosey. Is everyone all right? The gardener asked.

Yes we are fine. We are going to have to leave this planet. You are more then welcome to come with us. Rosey said.

Yes I think I will do that. The gardener answered.

Well go and get what you want to bring with you. And meet us at the spaceship. Nevis said.

I will go in and grab a few things too. Rosey said.

The maid came out at that. time rubbing her head. Rosey ran up to her. Are you ok? Rosey asked.

Yes but I have a headache from the shelves falling on me. The maid answered. What does it look *like* in there Rosey asked the *maid?*

It is a mess and unsafe to go in. The staircase is about to fall in and the rooms upstairs are going to fall down. The maid answered.

Well you are not going back in there. Nevis said.

But I have to get my pictures of Shavoth. I won't leave with out them. And some of the baby's things Rosey said.

You stay here I will go and get all those things. Nevis said. Took off in the palace.

Boy I really made a mess. Nevis said as he walked through the house.

Re climbed what was left of the staircase. It was creaking with every step he took.

Nevis made it up to his room. Grabbed a box and fill it up with pictures and the baby's thing. He went to the dresser and grabbed the book of spells out of the drawer. Then he climbed down the stairs as slow as he could.

Halfway down the stairs the bolts started coming loose. Nevis started running down the stairs. All at once the staircase started falling. Nevis went tumbling down the stairs.

The box flew out of his hands. When he stood up he reached down to start picking up the things that fell out of the box. Oh that hurts. Nevis looked at his leg and there was a board from the staircase sticking all the way through his leg. He put the things back in the box. He picked up one of the boards and used it as a crutch and started hobbling out of the palace the upstairs started to come down all around him.

Nevis tired to run out of the palace. As he made it out the palace started falling down around him.

Rosey came running up to Nevis. She grabbed the box and put her arm around Nevis and helped him to sit down on the bench in the garden.

This is all my fault. I should have never let you go back in there. Rosey said. Go get the gardener. Rosey looked at the maid then at Nevis's leg.

I am so sorry Nevis. Rosey said.

That's ok. Nevis said moaning in pain.

The gardener came running to see if everyone was all right. Oh my! You got yourself into it this time. The gardener said.

The maid came back I can't find the gardener. Then stopped. He's here now. Rosey said.

The gardener looked at Nevis this is going to hurt but it has to come out. You need to lie down on the ground. I need both of your help the gardener looked at Rosey and the maid. You hold is arms the and you hold his legs. The gardener said to the maid and Rosey.

Rosey grabbed Nevis's arm and the maid grabbed his legs.

I am so sorry Nevis I shouldn't have let you go in there. Rosey said.

That's ok I would have done anything for you. I love you so much. Nevis said. When Nevis and Rosey where talking the butler pulled the board out of Nevis's leg. Nevis started screaming. It took all Rosey and the maid's strength to hold him down.

I am not done yet the gardener said as Rosey went to let go.

Rosey looked at the maid. Will you check on the baby she is crying? The maid went over to the baby and picked her up.

I need to go to the stables and get some medicine and something to get these splinters out. The gardener said.

That hurt worse then getting shot. Nevis said. He was holding Rosey now. The gardener came back with the things that he needed.

Now this is going to hurt again as he poured water and washed the wound. I need to get all these splinters out before it gets infected. The gardener said.

Well hurry up. Nevis turned his head look at our home its in ruins. Nevis said. There was dust flying all over the place. Bricks and boards were laying all over the place.

When the gardener was done taking all the slivers out he put some salve and bandage on the wound. Well this is done the gardener said.

Where is your cane? Rosey asked.

I think I left it in the garden a few weeks ago. Nevis said. The gardener took off to look for it.

As Rosey helped Nevis to his feet. He tried to put pressure on his leg but couldn't. We cant go any where until your leg is better. Rosey said.

We are going to have to go we have no home left and there is nothing to hold us here anymore now. I will be ok grabbing Rosey's hand and kissing it.

We have our son to keep us here. Rosey said.

Yes but he will not leave Tarah and she will not leave this planet. Nevis said

I guess your right. I will go with you anywhere you want me to go but I sure wish we could see if Shavoth wants to go with. Rosey said.

The gardener came back with the cane. And handed it to Nevis. Thank you for helping me. Nevis told the gardener.

You are very welcome my friend. The gardener said.

Will you get everything together so we can leave. Nevis asked.

It will be my pleasure. The gardener said. And took off to get everything he could.

Nevis used the cane to pull himself up. And started hopping on one leg. Well lets go get in the spaceship. Nevis said.

The maid carried the baby and Rosey was carrying a box holding onto Nevis so he wouldn't fall.

They walked towards the spaceship. The baby started crying. Nevis looked at Rosey I can get in the spaceship by myself go take care of our daughter. Took the baby then handed the box to the maid. When Nevis could see that Rosey had the baby he said a spell and the trees started falling down around them. We must hurry Nevis said. As he tried to pick up his pace.

The gardener caught up to them dragging a wagon behind him, well I guess there wont be anything left of this planet real soon.

I know it was nice here until now. Nevis said.

Nevis started having a hard time walking so the gardener grabbed him by the arm lean on me for support. He said.

They all walked into the spaceship. Rosey hesitated on going inside. She turned around and looked at the grounds of the palace. The trees were falling down all over the place. And the ground was sucking everything in. she started crying. I don't know if I can leave without our son. She started crying.

It will be ok. Nevis said.

Can we at least stop and say goodbye. Rosey asked. Yes we can. Nevis said.

They all went inside.

The gardener was dragging the wagon in it was so full he had a hard time pulling it and holding onto Nevis at the same time.

Show them where they need to go, Nevis looked at the gardener.

The gardener took Rosey and the maid to their rooms. Made sure they were comfortable went and took the wagon and put things away then he went to help Nevis.

Nevis was starting up the spaceship. Weill guess we will really have to leave. The gardener said.

All of a sudden some of the knights ran up to the spaceship. Nevis looked out let them in we could use there help. Nevis said. The gardener went and opened the hatch and the knights came running in.

Everything is disappearing out there. They said.

The gardener closed the hatch.

All I want is my family safe so we are going to have to leave now. Nevis said.

Then he pushed a button on the panel and the spaceship started up. Then he pushed some more buttons and the spaceship went up in the air.

Nevis pushed some more buttons and set a course for earth. Well we wont be able to stop and see our son if the planet is falling apart lets hope they got off the planet Nevis said.

Elphany grabbed the microphone and instructed everyone to sit down and put their seatbelts on. The Joe and her went in and sat down in the captains chairs then buckled up.

Elphany started talking to the computer that Jahdson had installed for ber and ordered the spaceship where to go. As she pushed some buttons to start the engines.

Then put on the headphones and called for Jahdson.

I am right here. Jahdson said.

Do you have everyone ready? Elphany asked.

Yes we are all set everyone is in his or her places. Jahdson. Well then lets start the count down. Elphany said.

They all counted backwards from ten to one. Lets set of towards earth. Elphany said.

When they were in the air Elphany said ok Jahdson you can tell everyone they can get up and walk around. Call me if you have any problem son. Elphany said.

Ok will do mom. He said.

When they were almost in space Elphany went to the window and commanded the spaceship to open the slider so they could see out the window.

As the slider opened. Tarah and Shavoth walked up to Elphany and Joe. They flew over Nevis's palace, it was destroyed.

Can we go down and see if my mother is still there? Shavoth asked.

Elphany nodded got on the intercom to tell everyone what they were doing and to sit down and buckle up. As she was getting ready to order the spaceship to set down. All of a sudden there was an explosion. We have to get out of here now. Elphany yelled.

Elphany ordered the spaceship to go into space.

What about my mother? Shavoth asked.

I am truly sorry about your mother, baby sister and everyone else on Pholigue. But if we set down now we will all die. Joe said.

Elphany got on the speaker, let us all pray for those who stayed on Pholigue. There was complete silence for twenty minutes.

Shavoth put his hands over his eyes and started crying.

Succoth came running in in excitement. Running back and forth. What is it boy? Tarah asked.

He motioned for Tarah to follow him.

Well I guess we have to see what he wants. Come on everyone Tarah said looking at everyone. She held her hand out for Shavoth.

Shavoth dried his eyes and followed. Everyone out to where Succoth was going.

When they all walked into where Succoth went. There in the comer of the room was four little kittens.

Oh how cute. Tarah ran over to the kittens. You little sneak looking at Succoth laughing as she bent down to look at the kittens.

May I pick one up Tarah asked the mother. The mother shook her head yes. Tarah picked up one looked at it then did the same to the rest. When she got to the last one she said I guess you are the father looking at Succoth this one looks just like you Tarah said as she held the kitten up to Succoth.

Succoth licked the kitten in the face. Well I guess we better leave you two alone to get to know your babies. Tarah put the baby back with its mother. Got up and walked out of the room everyone followed.

Well there is a new beginning for our life. Tarah said.

Yes I think we are going to have a better life then having to worry about what Nevis is going to do next. Elphany said.

I just hope that your mother got off the planet in time. Joe said. And we will look around on earth to see if she did. Elphany said.

That I hope and if she did I will search all over for her till I do and keep her away from Nevis. I don't ever want to see him again. Shavoth said.

All we can do is pray that your mother and a lot more got out safely. Will we still have our powers on earth? Tarah asked looking at her mother.

Yes we will we ever we go our powers go with us. Elphany said. And Nevis will he have his? Tarah asked.

No his powers does not come from inside him. And he will lose them once he leave Pholigue.

So if Nevis got off Pholigue and he is headed towards earth the he has already lost all of his powers. So things will be normal for us finally. Joe said.

All four of them walked up to the window and looked out to the stars.

Well this is going to be the beginning of a new life for everyone on these two spaceships.

We have to figure out what to do with everyone and where he or she is going to live. Elphany said. Well I was thinking that we can build a big toy factory. And put them all to work. Joe said. that's a great idea but how are we going to make the people on earth believe that they have been there all their life's? Elphany said.

Like we did, remember. Joe said.

Well we still need to talk to everyone right now. Elphany said. She went over and put her headset on. Jahdson are you there?

Yes mom I am right here. Have you seen the star? Jahdson asked. Yes I have it is so beautiful out in space. Elphany answered.

I have decided I am going to be an when I get older. Jahdson said. And what's that? She asked.

An astronaut. He replied. that's good I am proud of you. Can you please turn your speaker on so I can talk to everyone. Elphany said. Jahdson turned the speaker on. Everyone listen my mom has something to say to all of you. Ok everyone is here go ahead.

I hope everyone has made the right decision on coming with us. And this is going to be very strange for all of you at first but we have figured something out for everyone of you. And the ones who want to go out on your own. I wish you well on whatever you do after we land on earth. There is something I need to ask each and everyone of you before we get to earth.

Please do not tell any of the people there where you come from if you do it could be very dangerous for all of us. Look inside your nightstand by your bed. This is for you to start a new life. Please use them wisely and you will have to change them for money, and you can see there is no returning to Pholigue ever. So I wish all of you the best in your new life's on earth. And the people there look the same as we do. And for most of them they are really nice people.

And I repeat do not let anyone know you are from another planet I love all of you very much.

Elphany finished by saying have a wonderful new life to all of you. And I will be waiting when we land to see all of you off.

They both turned their speakers off. You know mom everyone on this spaceship wants to go where we are going they really love being with you. Jahdson said. that's wonderful son we are going to have to find a big area to land these spaceships then we will see what everyone wants to do. Now you need to get something to eat. And I will see you and everyone else when we touch down on earth. Elphany said.

Ok mom I am a little hungry. And thank you for going back home. Jahdson said. I love you son. She told him.

And I love you dad Tarah and Shavoth. Jahdson told his mom.

Ok now lets go eat I think I can vouch for everyone here that we are all hungry. Joe said. That sounds good Tarah are you and Shavoth going to join us? Elphany asked.

Tarah looked at Shavoth. There was a sad look on his face. You two go ahead we will be there before to long. Tarah said looking at Shavoth.

Alright we will be in the dining area with the rest of the people here when you are ready. I will have the cook hold a couple of plates for you. But don't be to long ok. Elphany said.

Elphany and Joe walked out of the room, down the corridor and disappeared

Tarah grabbed Shutout's hand. I am really truly sorry about your mom and little sister Shavoth your mom was a beautiful woman. Tarah said.

Thank you but I feel that deep down inside that they aren't really gone so hopefully everyone is right she got off of Pholigue in time. And I feel that she is so close to me. Shavoth said.

Yes I am feeling the same way its like there is something wrong here but I cannot pin it down yet and with everything that has happened and all these people here are overwhelmed right now I don't want to say or do anything to upset anyone right now we just need to keep our eyes open. Tarah said.

Well maybe we should tell your parents just in case so they can be aware. Shavoth said.

You know if Nevis got off the planet then he most likely has your mom and sister with him and he is on his way to earth as we speak. Tarah said.

You could be right Shavoth eyes sparkled a little when Tarah said that. Well lets just focus on them being on their way to earth then. And I think we need to let your parents know about the feelings that we are having. So lets go eat I am a little hungry now.

They both walked down the corridor into the dining area. Boy this spaceship is really big. Shavoth said. The corridor was twelve high and it was twelve feet or more wide.

And yellow and blue lights inside the ceiling and floors.

They both walked towards the dining area. There were a lot of long tables with benches by them.

Tarah and Shavoth walked up to the line of people. Shavoth took two of the trays from the person that was handing them out. He handed one tray to Tarah and followed the crowd to the counter. Picked the food and drinks they wanted. Looking around to find a place to sit.

Hey there are two seats next to Lavasco. Tarah said.

They walked over and sat down. Well you are awful quite. Tarah said looking at Lavasco.

I am just worried on how everyone is going to except me on this new planet earth. And Rosey is gone. Lavasco said.

Well as far as people excepting you on earth you don't have anything to worry about you are a very handsome man. And as far as my mother I feel deep down inside that she is still alive. And I am going to look for her as soon as we get to earth. Shavoth said.

Thanks you are making me feel a little better. And I will go with you I am going to get her away from Nevis. I should have done it years ago when you were a baby. Lavasco said.

Elphany and Joe walked up to them. You wont be able to carry your sword around or any other weapon like that on earth no on there does. And we are going to have to figure out how to get everyone new clothes cause the one they are wearing are so much different then what we have on. Elphany said.

Why don't we just have them altered? Joe asked.

Sounds good [will tell everyone about it. Elphany said.

When you guys are done eating can you join us to watch the stars. Joe said. Then Elphany and Joe they walked over to talk to Robert, Stan and tripper.

Have you three decided what you are going to do when you get to earth. Joe asked.

Well Robert. has a lot of explaining to do with his wife. And Tripper is going to stay at my house. I can get him a job on the police force with Robert and me. Or maybe a private investigation business into looking up what we went through.

That sounds good. Robert and Tripper said. that's really great and good luck to you Robert. Joe shook their hands, said good luck.

Elphany and Joe walked out of the dining room, down the corridor and back into the front of the spaceship to watch the stars.

When they walked in there. Joe grabbed Elphany and wrapped his arms around her. You know I am really worried about all these people we had brought with us. Elphany said.

They will be all right look how we were when we were there we adjusted really good. And we don't have to worry about Nevis doing anything either. He lost his powers when he left Pholigue. That's if he did get off in time. Joe said.

I hope that he got Rosey and the baby off too. For Shavoth sake. But all those other people that didn't want to come with us. Are they all gone. Elphany said. And started crying.

Well they are at peace with god now and all we can do is pray that they didn't suffer. Joe said. Your right as usual. Elphany said.

Tarah, Shavoth and Lavasco all walked In at the same time.

Will you two take that somewhere else. Looking at Elphany and Joe hugging each other. Lavasco said. Well we are going to have to find Lavasco a wife aren't we. Elphany said with a big grin on her face. Lavasco didn't say a word his face showed it all he was blushing from ear to ear.

Lets watch as the stars go by. Elphany said. They are so beautiful. This is so romantic. Tarah said. Shavoth came up behind Tarah and wrapped his arms around her. Whispered in her ear. I love you so much. And kissed her on the neck.

The reason why we asked you all here is because I was wondering what you are going to do when we get to earth. Elphany said.

We thought you three could stay with us for awhile until you can find your own place. We are going to build a toy factory and we would like Shavouth and Lavasco help get run it.

That sound great Lavasco said.

And I would like to start a restaurant with all different types of food on the menu. I would like you to help me with that Tarah.

Sounds great to me. But what about all the rest of the people we are going to help them get into their own place and Joe is going to put some of them to work at the toy factory and maybe some at the restaurant. And well some will probably go on there own. We all will make sure they will have everything they need. As far as us we have enough gems with us to live comfortably the rest of our life's and so will our kids, our grandkids and so on. Elphany said.

But as for all of us here and Jahdson we will always be a family and no on will ever try and separate up again no matter what. Joe said.

And we have this rare gift from god that could change the whole universe for the good of god. Our powers will never be used for any kind of evil at all. And we will make sure that we will stop evil where it stands. Elphany was looking at Tarah.

And I will be right beside you every step of the way. Shavouth said.

We will all be together every step of the way the love we have for each other cannot be broken and that includes you Lavasco no matter what you are a part of this family and we ware going to give you our last name. which is Sherman. I know of someone that can give all three of you a birth certificate.

So now we have to figure out you an Torah's last name. Elphany said looking at Shavouth.

How about Gardener Shavouth and Tarah gardener. Because Tarah loves to sit in the middle of the garden flowers. Shavouth said and bent down and kissed Tarah on the lips.

That is so true when she was a baby and Joe and I went out to the patio all the time that is where she would end up even before she could walk she would find a way to go in there. Elphany said.

This is a new beginning for us. We will never give up on each other we are one big happy family. Elphany went over to the headset and put it on Jahdson are you there.

I am right here mom I am watching the stars. Jahdson said.

And so are we. Lavasco is going to stay with all of us for awhile or however long he wants. And we decided to give him our last name. Elphany said.

Sounds good to me Jahdson said.

What I want you to do is hold your right hand up in the air and repeat after me. We are one united as we are and we will be one united forever let no other being separate us from each other. Elphany said.

Ok everyone do as you mom says Joe said.

They all held up their right hand and said at the same time we are one united as we are and we will be one united forever let no other being separate us from each other.

They all fell silent after that looking out the window watching the star eager to start a new life and wondering what lies ahead of them.

This will forever change them but will this be the beginning of a new life or will it start when they left the planet Pholigue.

And where is Nevis is he right behind them ahead of them or was he on the planet Pholigue when it blew up? Only time will tell and they will have a whole lifetime to find out.

But either way it goes they will be there by each other to stop evil before it happens.

The End